PARANOR

Stiffs & Petroglyphs

TRIXIE SILVERTALE

Sittin' On A Goldmine
Productions L.L.C.

Sittin' On A Goldmine Productions, L.L.C.

info@sittinonagoldmine.co

www.sittinonagoldmine.co

ISBN: 978-1-952739-63-7

Cover Design © Sittin' On A Goldmine Productions, L.L.C.

Cover design by Melony Paradise of Paradise Cover Design

Trixie Silvertale
Stiffs and Petroglyphs: Paranormal Cozy Mystery : a novel / by
Trixie Silvertale — 1st ed.
[1. Paranormal Cozy Mystery — Fiction. 2. Cozy Mystery —

Fiction. 3. Amateur Sleuths — Fiction. 4. Private Investigator — Fiction. 5. Wit and Humor — Fiction.] 1. Title.

CHAPTER 1

I'VE EXPERIENCED A MYRIAD of strange goings on since my arrival in almost-Canada, but nothing surpasses the hubbub that accompanies the annual cleaning of the Bell, Book & Candle's tin-plated ceiling. As part of the "pre" prep, my volunteer employee Twiggy is bossing us around.

"Gusse Pierce is the only guy in the tri-state area that still has the necessary skill to properly maintain this vintage tin. I won't have Pyewacket hissing at him or stealing his lunch!"

Twiggy stands between the stacks on the first floor, while Pyewacket, my half-wild caracal, perches atop of one of the dark wooden bookcases in all his tan glory. His black-tufted ears twitch at the sound of his name, and his short, thick tail flicks once. "Reeeee-ow." A warning.

My grandmother's best friend, in life, Twiggy shakes her finger toward our furry overlord. "Did you hear that? That's just the kind of thing I can't have happening when Gusse is here."

Leaning on the thick balustrade bordering the curved second-floor mezzanine that houses our most rare tomes, I attempt to rain down some sympathy. "I hear what you're saying, Twiggy, but I can't keep Pyewacket locked in the walk-up! He has secret passages everywhere. No matter what I do, he's bound to find a way out."

"That's why I keep telling you to take him out to my cabin!" Twiggy stomps one of her biker-boot-clad feet for emphasis and flicks her severe grey pixie cut as she glares at me. "The weather is perfect. The leaves might even be turning out there. You only have to stay for a couple of days and everything will be done."

The last time I attempted a trip out to Twiggy's cabin with my fiendish feline, we uncovered a cold case involving a vengeful spirit, but that's another story. "Look, it's not just me anymore. I have to talk to Erick. If we're working on a case, that's a long drive we probably don't want to deal with."

She plants a fist on her hip. "Is Isadora here, kid?"

Myrtle Isadora is my not-as-dead-as-everyone-thinks grandmother. She and her alchemist/lawyer

Silas Willoughby discovered a way to tether her spirit to the bookshop — permanently. Twiggy can neither see nor hear my grandmother's ghost. However, I am blessed with both. So I slip off my proverbial private investigator hat and pop on my afterlife interpreter cap. "Grams, do you have anything helpful to contribute?"

My classy grandmother smooths her burgundy silk-and-tulle Marchesa burial gown and adjusts one of her many strands of pearls. "Sorry, sweetie. Pyewacket is your responsibility now."

Throwing my hands in the air, I walk across the thick carpets of the Rare Books Loft and head down the wrought-iron circular staircase. "She's here, and she's not helping!"

It's a testament to Twiggy's commitment to finding a solution that she unhooks the chain at the bottom, which restricts access and supports the "No Admittance" sign.

I rush past before the alarm is triggered, and she reconnects the chain.

"Look, Twiggy, you know how important you are to running this bookshop. I'll talk to Erick about it. Maybe we could all go over to his old house. He still hasn't put it on the market."

She shoves her hands deep into the pockets of her dungarees and scoffs. "That's because he's as smart as he is handsome. The market is terrible right now. Might as well hang on to that thing until property values start going up. I suppose he's in no rush to sell now that he's married to an heiress." Her cackle echoes off the dusty tin-plated ceiling.

"Oh, hilarious. Don't you dare say that to him. He's very sensitive about our financial imbalance."

Grams rushes toward me. On her way, she passes directly through the massive chandelier above us. "You should give him an allowance, dear. Maybe that would help."

My laughter joins Twiggy's continuing cackle, and it takes a moment for me to catch my breath. "Sometimes I wonder how you managed to work your way through so many husbands, and then you say something like that. 'Give him an allowance.' That's when it all becomes crystal clear!"

Twiggy's eyes nearly pop out of her head when I report my grandmother's recommendation. Our laughter continues in unison.

Ghost-ma takes immediate offense. "Well, I never!"

Without skipping a beat, I toss out my standard retort. "We both know that's not true, don't we? Myrtle Isadora Johnson Linder Duncan Willamet Rogers."

The phone tucked in the back pocket of my skinny jeans rings out and puts a temporary pause on our conversation

Out of habit, I answer on speaker. I'm very accustomed to having no secrets in an environment where my grandmother's ghost can drop in on my thoughts at will, and my volunteer employee seems to have up-to-the-minute gossip about anything and everything that goes on in my life. It's actually how she allows me to compensate her — hilarious stories about my many mishaps, rather than a check.

"Go for Mitzy."

A hesitant voice on the other end responds. "Hello. Is this Mitzy Moon?"

My mind instantly goes to the snarky. How many Mitzys does this guy know? But before I can utter my reply, an auditory memory tickles my grey matter. For a moment I feel as though I'm in one of those movie scenes where the director has chosen to rapidly zoom in on the subject while simultaneously changing the depth of field. Creating a radical shrinking feeling.

I could never forget that voice!

When I worked as a pretty-much-broke barista in Sedona, Arizona, the commands of my supervisor Dean featured prominently in my nightmares. Dean was always super positive. He had all sorts of new-age woo woo phrases and constantly pushed us all to be our best selves. He threw around the word "super" like it alone had the power to heal the world. So we ended up calling him our SUPERvisor . . . Emphasis on super.

Twiggy snaps her fingers in front of my face, and my eyes widen. Classic me! The film school dropout in me took over, and I drifted into one of my mind movies. "Sorry, yes. This is Mitzy Moon."

"Well, hello, Mitzy. It's Dean. I'm not sure if you remember me. I was your supervisor at Hot Kafka in Sedona."

No need to share my mental miniseries with him. "Oh, hello, Dean. Great to hear from you. Any particular reason for your call?"

He clears his throat, and I can practically see him adjusting his ridiculous man bun. "I got your number from Benicio Alvarez. He designed a large custom landscaping project here in Sedona and came in for coffee. I happened—"

"You can skip the back story, Dean. Why are you calling me?" I'm struggling to keep the irritation from my voice. This man pushed my buttons for the better part of a year before Silas Willoughby showed up at the door of my should-have-been-condemned apartment, looked me straight in the eyes, and handed me a manila envelope with a future that continues to get brighter.

"Yes, sorry. My girlfriend is missing."

I take a deep breath, patiently waiting for additional information.

None comes.

"I'm sorry to hear that, Dean. Although, I'm still not sure why you're calling me." It's great to see that some things never change.

"Oh, of course. When I was reconnecting with Benicio, he mentioned something about you solving crimes. I was hoping I could hire you."

"You realize I don't live in Arizona anymore, right, Dean?"

"Of course. I visualized you driving out . . . or maybe you could fly? Whatever works. I just thought maybe you had some friends you could visit—"

"Dean. Let's not worry about planning my trip just yet. Why don't you call the local police?"

"Oh, didn't I mention? She was attending a sweat lodge ceremony on Native land. The local law enforcement has no jurisdiction."

"All right. And have you driven out there to look for her yourself?"

"Of course. That was the first thing I did when she didn't show up. Everyone at the retreat center claimed she'd had some spiritual breakthrough and left early. But I've been calling her phone. She's not answering. I've gone to her apartment, and she's not there."

A large part of me thinks that her spiritual breakthrough might have revealed Dean to be highly annoying and convinced her she'd be better off without him, but I don't say that. "Are you sure she didn't just turn off her phone?"

"Well, for the first few days it was ringing, and now it's not. I think something bad happened. It's a feeling in my heart chakra. You know how I get those."

Grams snickers behind me, reminding me that the entire call has been on speakerphone. Twiggy nods her head encouragingly.

"Let me talk to my partner and check our schedule, Dean. I'll call you back in about an hour. Does that work?"

"Oh, that would be great. I would be super grateful if you could make this work. Thank you for—"

"I'll talk to you later, Dean." I can tell how serious the situation is by the fact that he only tossed one superfluous "super" into our entire conversation.

Looks like I'll be trotting down Main Street to the official offices of Harper and Moon Investigations to talk to my hubby. Who knows? He might be SUPER interested in a trip to Arizona.

CHAPTER 2

BEFORE I HEAD OUT, my grandmother retrieves a stack of 3 x 5 index cards and a pen. She and Twiggy will continue to debate the finer points of how to best protect the workers from the fangs and claws of our territorial caracal via the notecard system.

I open the heavy wooden door of my bookshop and step onto the sidewalk at the corner of First and Main.

Turning right, I head down First Avenue toward my office. I feel like such an important and grown-up individual. I have an *office*. I've come a long way, baby!

However, that call from my old boss inevitably sends me tumbling down memory lane. If I aim to avoid a shame spiral, I better act fast.

Pausing on the sidewalk, I gaze up at the bookshop, soak in the tableau, and smile. I never pictured this future. I wanted to get out of the coffee-slinging business and pay my bills on time, but when I used to try to imagine such a future — everything was black.

A great nothingness of failure.

Hopefully, I'll never forget how lucky I am and how important it is to give back to my community. It's also pretty awesome that my husband, Erick Harper, shares my penchant for philanthropy.

As I traipse past my father's Restorative Justice Foundation, a gentle breeze rolls up from the great lake nestled in the harbor behind my bookshop. There's a subtle whiff of the impending change of season in the wind.

The sun overhead is warm, but it's lost the intensity of midsummer. As we head toward the fall equinox, the temperatures in Pin Cherry Harbor slowly drop and the warmth of the sun holds more comfort than punishment. There's also a noticeable reduction in humidity, which definitely sits well with this desert girl.

It shouldn't be a problem to convince Erick to head to Arizona again. Not that Dean and I were actually friends, but sometimes I miss the Southwest and the red rocks of Sedona. If we can help

Dean find some peace of mind while we're in town, so be it.

The old gas station converted into our new office comes into view, and I cross the street eagerly.

When I pull the front door open, my husband's dreamy blue eyes look up with too much hope.

"Sorry, Harper. Just me."

He hops up from the partners desk we share and strides across the small office to greet me. Stopping a step away, he glances at my T-shirt and laughs. "It really is like you're having these custom made."

I shrug and tug at the hem. Today's shirt says, "All I care about are Fries and like 3 people." Erick is on to something, though. "Actually, Grams and Pye picked this up in one of their unauthorized online shopping sprees. I'm pretty sure it's one of a kind."

He nods and walks closer. "Now, where was I? Oh, right. Don't sell yourself short, Moon. It's always a pleasure to see you." He scoops me into his arms and kisses me softly.

"My, my, my. If I'd known that office jobs could be this rewarding, I would've gotten one a long time ago."

We share a snicker and he offers me a seat on the sofa in our pseudo waiting room. "Can I get you a cup of coffee?"

I flash my eyebrows and grin. "You know me so well."

He walks toward the back room and I admire the cut of his jib, or rather his perfectly fitting jeans.

Erick returns a couple of minutes later with two cups of coffee. Black for him, and cream only for me.

"No chocolate croissants?"

He stops for a moment and hangs his head, before taking a seat next to me on the leather, flared-arm sofa. "To be honest, I had breakfast at Myrtle's Diner, and Odell tossed a couple of extra pancakes on my plate. I'm completely stuffed. I may skip lunch."

I nearly launch a spit take, but I'm somehow able to swallow my coffee before I respond. "Skip lunch? Never heard of it. I don't think I'd like it."

He bumps his knee against mine and grins. "You wouldn't." Erick takes a long sip of coffee, and a sweet sparkle lights his face. "There must be a reason you walked all the way down here, Moon."

"And there it is." I lift my cup of coffee in a mock toast. "Former Sheriff Harper using his people skills to decipher my body language. Mad respect."

He takes a seated bow and tilts his head. "Spill, Moon."

"All right. You got me. My old supervisor Dean called this morning."

"Late for your shift, eh?" He chuckles at his own lame joke.

"I'm laughing on the inside, where it counts." Blerg. "Try again."

Erick leans back, sighs, and his eyes dart back and forth in his head. "Let's see . . . Dean . . . He's the one from Hot Kafka, right? When we went there, it was called something else. But he's the guy that always thinks everything is *super*. Am I right?"

"Very good, Mr. Harper. If you remember anniversaries and birthdays as well as you remember trivia about my life, I'll consider myself a lucky woman."

His lips curve into a crooked grin and he shrugs. "I thought you already considered yourself a lucky woman."

Oh brother. "Look, Detective Too-Hot-To-Handle, we don't have time to stroke your ego this morning. Dean's girlfriend went missing on Native land and we need to decide if we're going to fly all the way to Arizona to help him out."

Erick asks a series of typically rational questions, and I have answers to about half of them. Eventually we get around to the fact that neither of us has a boss to report to and my grandmother's estate left me enough cash to fly wherever I want, whenever I want, with whomever I want.

"So, I'll take care of booking the flights and you figure out what kind of car you'd like to rent when we land in Flagstaff."

"Flagstaff? But last time we flew into Phoenix."

"Last time we were going to the Southwest to solve my mother's cold case. My mom and I lived in Phoenix until she passed away, and then I got shoved into the foster system. As I worked my way across the state, from one foster family to another, I eventually ended up in northern Arizona. And when I finally liberated myself from that whole she-bang, I landed in Sedona. Flagstaff is closer to the potential case."

Erick sets his empty coffee mug on the small maple table in front of the couch and smiles. "And by liberated I'm guessing you mean ran away. Correct?"

"Listen, Officer, I don't want any trouble. I was practically eighteen, and I made my way just fine. No point dwelling on the past."

He chuckles. "Mitzy Moon at seventeen. I'm certainly glad I didn't have to tame that delinquent."

"Rude."

His warm laughter fills the small space, and he slips an arm around my shoulders. "Hey, trust me when I tell you, I'm not one to cast stones. We all made some less than stellar decisions in our youth. Right?"

Leaning against him, I inhale his citrus-woodsy scent and smile. "You're not wrong."

"So we're headed west!" Erick inhales sharply. "You'd better call Howie Fairlane, the Great White North's only IT Specialist, and make sure that your Phoom system is working. I don't want the ghost of your grandmother coming after us for abandoning her."

"Good point! Pyewacket and Grams will be miffed as it is when they find out we'll be working on a case without them."

Erick holds up a finger. "Well, if you get that video conferencing portal working, we won't be doing it without them — technically."

"Another excellent point. Seems like I have a few things to take care of. Travel arrangements. IT stuff . . . and enduring a probably endless packing session with Grams!"

His nearness brings a heat to my cheek as he plants a kiss. "Don't forget to pack sleepwear."

At first, his comment makes no sense, but when I see the lascivious look in his eye, I gasp. "Don't you dare mention lingerie within earshot of Ghost-ma! She's liable to blow her otherworldly circuits if she gets wind of you requesting sexy sleepwear. You know how she keeps going on and on about great-grandchildren!"

Erick lifts both of his hands in the air as though I'm holding the gun in a Wild West stick up. "Hey, I didn't say anything about grandchildren. But it's not often we get to take off on our own, and I thought maybe we could count this as a second honeymoon."

"Nice try, Harper. We're flying out to Arizona on a case. So, that's officially work. And I seem to remember you giving a little speech about not mixing work and pleasure."

He gets to his feet, offers me a hand, and, as he pulls me up, his arms circle around my waist and hold me tight. "That's the problem, Moon. Every day I work with you is a pleasure."

Oh brother.

CHAPTER 3

ERICK OFFERS TO STAY at the office and research tribal law enforcement in Arizona. That sounds about as exciting as watching grass grow, so I head back to the bookshop to break the news of our trip to Grams and see if I can get an appointment with Howie Fairlane.

Pin Cherry Harbor is definitely the town that tech forgot, but for the handful of folks who venture into the virtual there's only one man for the job.

"Hey, Howie, it's Mitzy Moon. Oh, I'm fine, thanks for asking. What? No, we don't need another closed-circuit TV venture." Forcing a laugh, I struggle to get this greased pig of a conversation back on track. "I need you to run a quick check of that video conferencing system you installed. Yes, the Phoom system. You guessed it. Just another trip for world traveler Mitzy Moon." He's killing me with this small talk. "Today? That's fast. Sure. What time—" Howie launches into another bit from his imagined standup routine and I bite my tongue. "You got it. I'll see you when I see you."

"Mitzy, are you leaving?"

Back in the day, Grams used to get a real kick out of sneaking up on me to see if she could cause any pants accidents. Since I can always see and hear her, the idea that she could surprise me gave her quite a thrill. Now that we've been together for a few years, I've learned to recognize her energetic signature — in all its sneaky forms.

"Well, you don't have to spoil my fun, sweetie. You could pretend to be surprised."

"But wouldn't you know the difference?"

She shrugs her designer-gown-clad shoulders. "I can pretend too."

"How about we simply skip ahead to the part where I tell you the less than great news?"

A bejeweled hand covers her mouth as she gasps. "Trouble in paradise? Did you do something to upset Erick?"

My mouth hangs open like a broken mailbox. "Oh, fantastic. If something goes wrong with Erick, you immediately assume it would be my fault."

Twiggy stomps out of the back room. "I'm only

catching half of it, but if we're choosing sides, I'm team Erick."

Throwing my arms in the air, I shout into the empty bookshop. "What did I ever do?"

Grams and Twiggy both chuckle in their own dimensions, although Twiggy's laugh is always closer to a cackle.

Climbing over the chain at the bottom of the wrought-iron circular staircase, I head up to the Rare Books Loft. "Howie Fairlane is on his way over, Twiggy. Will you send him up to the apartment when he gets here?"

She crosses her arms and gazes at the second floor mezzanine. "I guess that means you're headed to Arizona. You and Erick decided to take the case, eh?"

"We did. I'm actually going to give my dad a call to let him know I'll be out of town, but I can ask him if he'd be willing to watch Pyewacket. Amaryllis loves that little demon spawn."

Twiggy claps her hands and offers me a mock salute. "Just when I thought you were gonna let me down, doll."

I grab the candle handle next to my hard-won copy of *Saducismus Triumphatus* and wait impatiently for the bookcase door to slide open. Ghostma hovers nervously beside me. "What are you waiting for, Grams? Usually you blast through the wall like it's nothing."

"I'm not myself, dear. I didn't want to worry you when I heard you'd be traveling, but my energy has been awfully low. I haven't been able to hold my quill pen or work on my memoirs for several days."

"I think you meant to say *my* memoirs. But I'll let it slide this time." I arch an eyebrow at the literal ghostwriter, as she attempts to paint her luminous features in the portrait of innocence.

"You're probably just bored. I have to pack for my trip. That should put a little spark in your spirit."

She zooms into the closet I've nicknamed *Sex and the City* meets *Confessions of a Shopaholic*, mumbling about weather in Arizona and potential undercover identities.

Taking a quick stroll around the apartment, I straighten the pillow on the settee and fluff the shams on the now unused king-sized bed.

Glancing at the telephone privacy booth in the corner, I push the wall and it pops open to reveal an old rotary phone and a small walnut bench. Thank goodness for cell phones. There are plenty of things I dislike about the miniature mobile computers, but being able to take them wherever you want and not be leashed to a claustrophobic booth like this makes perfect sense to me.

Ghost-ma calls out from the closet. "How many suitcases are you taking?"

I march into the closet with one fist firmly planted on my curvy hip. "One. One suitcase and one carry-on. So you better make your choices count, Isadora."

She ignores me completely and heads for one of the built-in drawers. "I'm sure you'll be needing one of these." She pulls out a lacy red-and-black teddy and shakes it back and forth.

"Grams! No lingerie! No exceptions. This is a work trip. Erick and I have a case to solve. I will take a bathing suit and some yoga wear, though. If we have to go undercover, we may be forced to endure a sweat lodge."

Her perfectly smooth brow creases. "Endure? I thought sweat lodges were very spiritual experiences?"

"I'll explain later. I have to call my dad about Pyewacket."

A quick call to my father reveals that he and Amaryllis are in Chicago. The huge deal they've been working on with the international shipping company is all coming together and they're signing papers and having a celebration. He suggests asking Silas, and I wonder why I didn't think of that first.

"Thanks, Dad. That's a great idea. Congratulations on the deal, and give Amaryllis a hug for me."

Next call, my mentor.

Flopping onto the antique, four-poster bed, I tap the speaker icon and place the phone on the bed beside me.

"Good morning. I trust you slept well, Mizithra."

"Hey, what's with the formal name?" Oops. "I mean, good morning, Mr. Willoughby. I trust you had a restful repose."

He chuckles, and I can picture his cheeks turning pink and his jowls jiggling.

"How may I assist, Mitzy?"

"Twiggy's looking for a cat sitter. They're starting the annual ceiling polish tomorrow and she needs Pyewacket off the premises."

"Ah. Is there a reason you are unable to take our feline friend to her cabin?"

"There is. Erick and I are headed to Arizona. An old boss of mine has a girlfriend that went missing at a sweat lodge ceremony on Native land."

There's no reply, but I know better than to interrupt this silent thought interval.

"Perhaps you should consult Nimkii out on Hawk Island. He is an elder of the local tribe and may be able to offer an introduction to the tribe you're visiting."

"I appreciate the thought, Silas, and while I will always defer to your expertise in alchemy, you have to trust me when it comes to Sedona. I'm willing to bet my entire estate that the shaman running these sweat lodges is no Native American. Sedona is filled with *white* shamans. They attend one hokey naming ceremony and the next thing you know, they're claiming to be an honorary member of some tribe or another. Sure, there are legitimate ceremonies and honest non-natives who support American Indian culture, but I'm pretty sure that's not who we'll be dealing with. I'm guessing this shaman will be named something utterly flippant, like Tracy or Skip."

Silas harrumphs. "I believe it to be a grave error to abuse the sacred. It is my sincere hope that what you're telling me is not what you discover. However, I, in fact, shall defer to your expertise in this area, Mitzy."

"Thanks. I'm not sure what we'll find, Silas. I'm hoping this woman simply left the retreat ahead of schedule and isn't answering Dean's calls. That would be ideal. But if it's something worse, like murder, do you have any words of wisdom for me?"

Again, I force myself to patiently sit through the quiet.

"I would highly recommend that you and Mr. Harper work on a detailed cover story. And I further advise your undercover identity not involve a hairpiece. If you must subject yourself to the cleansing heat of a sweat lodge, it would be most wise to do so without the burden of a wig."

"Excellent advice, Mr. Willoughby. And you are correct in assuming that Erick is joining me. If you wouldn't mind checking in on Grams while I'm gone, I'd appreciate it. You know how lonely she gets."

That comment brings a brief chuckle from my mentor. "Perhaps it would be best if I simply take up temporary residence in your old apartment. Then Pyewacket will be within a paw's reach of the video-conferencing system, and I can keep Isadora company."

"The Phoom thing-y! Pye will stalk me mercilessly if he doesn't have access to that." I exhale in relief. "I'm so glad you thought of that, Silas. You're welcome to make yourself at home in the apartment, or the walk-up, while we're gone. Um, can you deal with Twiggy? She's gonna be a little salty when she learns that he'll be 'in' the bookshop during the ceiling-cleaning fiasco."

"Twiggy is nothing if not practical. I look forward to conversing with her on this matter."

"Oh, are there any alchemical workings you need to teach me before I leave?"

"I must encourage you not to use any runes or

reversal symbols on sacred land. The energies that inhabit those spaces are delicate. The risk would not be worth the reward. However, I may have an item or two that you could safely employ. I shall check my stock and make a trip into town if I find anything that would genuinely assist your investigation."

"Thank you. We shouldn't be gone for more than a week. I'll keep you posted, and Howie—"

BING. BONG. BING.

Twiggy's voice crackles over the intercom. "Howie is here. Should I send him up?"

Rolling off the bed, I smooth the comforter and grab my phone as I rush toward the mother-of-pearl buttons on the wall near the secret door. "I better let you go, Silas. The IT guy is here to check the videoconferencing system. Thanks again."

"When do you depart?" His voice is tense, and I wonder if he had some kind of premonition of his own.

Before I can answer Silas, I have to depress the plaster medallion of twisted ivy that opens the secret door and then push the mother-of-pearl button on the left to reply to Twiggy. "Send him up."

"Sorry, Silas. We're gonna catch a flight out tomorrow. So, if you think of anything, bring it by tonight, all right?"

"Indeed."

Howie appears at the top of the circular stair-case, and no matter how many times I run into this guy, he always catches me off guard.

Howie Fairlane is not a stereotypical geek. Howie Fairlane is a leading man! If I were casting roles for a student film, this six-foot-four-inch Greek god would never in a million years play a computer nerd. His close-cropped black hair, rugged jaw, moose-sized shoulders, and bulging biceps scream "on-screen hero."

However, his wardrobe is nerd-adjacent. A short-sleeved polo shirt, white athletic socks with two red stripes around the calf, and polyester gym-teacher shorts from the 80s. "Well, if it isn't Mrs. Harper!"

"How are you doing, Howie? And it's Mrs. Moon."

"What? Are you trying to tell me Ricky took your last name?" Howie's broad forehead wrinkles in consternation.

"Nope. We each kept our own names. With all the legal stuff surrounding my grandmother's estate, it was simpler that way. And I like my name."

Howie shakes his head and rubs his thumb along the side of his nose. "Boy, oh boy, you modern kids. What can I do ya for?"

I better strap in and get ready for all his folksy quips that drive me nuts. This guy acts like he's twenty years older than me, even though he and Erick went to high school together. I'd like to ask if he's still single, but last time I asked that question, he thought I was interested.

"I just need you to make a quick check of the system you installed before." I lead him to the small desk and gesture to the setup. "It's right here. Can you make sure it's all working as simply as before?"

"If Howie Fairlane can't do it, nobody can."

His flirtatious smile and forgettable tagline almost ruin the view. Almost.

He grabs the keyboard and types furiously. "Oh boy, looks like you need a system update . . . Better do something about that firewall . . . There's a newer version of the app . . ."

"*How-to* Fairlane? I can't believe I'm finding you in my wife's apartment?" Erick Harper jokingly crosses his arms over his own impressive chest and tilts his head questioningly in Howie's direction.

"Ricky!" Howie's tree-trunk legs stride toward my husband. "Hey, that was a heckuva wedding you threw, Sheriff." The IT guy shakes Erick's hand vigorously and simultaneously pounds him on the back with his other meaty paw.

"Thanks. And I'm not the sheriff anymore, How-to. You know that."

My curiosity can only sit on standby for so long. "Remind me how you got the nickname How-to?"

Of course, I remember, but I'm eager to move away from the "sheriff" conversation.

Erick glances at me with a sly smile. "Howie got his nickname because he was always showing everyone on the football team 'how to' do the drills properly. He was definitely coach's favorite."

A broad grin spreads across Howie's chiseled features, and the room fills with an extra dose of testosterone. "I've been coaching football and baseball for almost ten years now." He jerks a thumb toward his shiny polo shirt. "Got my own favorites."

My "Howie meter" just hit the red zone. I need some air. "I'll let you get to work, Howie. I'll be downstairs helping Twiggy. Just come and find me when you finish."

"You got it, Mrs. Moon." He winks at Erick and chuckles like he's part of an inside joke.

Yeesh.

CHAPTER 4

WITH HOW-TO FAIRLANE out of the bookshop, it's time to procure the suitcases. And yes, I said *suitcases*, plural. I have little faith in Grams being able to pare down her choices. Luckily, Erick will happily tote whatever I have to take. One of the many things I love about that man.

As I walk through the children's section toward the hidden door, I straighten a few stuffed animals and smile when I catch sight of the new beanbag chair. What is it about beanbag chairs? They're the coolest things — until a certain age — and then they become some kind of trap.

Anyway, I hit the light on my phone to locate the well-hidden door.

As I approach the refurbished oak paneling, a smile creeps across my face. The last time I attempted to leave town for an extended trip, my seemingly aloof caracal scratched the door to kingdom come in an attempt to gain access and stowaway in one of the suitcases.

While my bookstore houses many secret doors and passages, turns out this little bugger is the most difficult to open that I've encountered since I moved into the bookshop and learned most of the lay of the land. You actually have to twist a small portrait hanging on the wall and depress a button hidden beneath an embossed header-strip of cloth wallpaper at the same time. If not for the intermittent aid of my enchanted vintage 70s mood ring with a smoky-black cabochon in the center of gold braided trim, I'm not sure I would've remembered the proper sequence.

Once I succeed in gaining access, I drag out two suitcases and begrudgingly make my way back up the spiral staircase.

You would think I'd have learned my lesson about the circular staircase, or, as it should be called, my nemesis. Clearly, I'm either a slow learner or just plain stubborn. Spoiler alert: it's the latter. I take a run at carrying both suitcases upstairs at the same time.

By now, I'm sure you've come to realize this won't end well for me.

One of the wheels catches on a metal stair. I

lose my balance and I tumble backward, landing on a suitcase, and then firmly on the first floor.

The dulcet tones of Twiggy's cackle are my sole reward. "Thanks for the show, kid. That should tide me over until you get back from your little sleuthing trip."

Getting to my feet, I dust off my backside, pick up one suitcase, and make a small curtsy. "No problem. Happy to pay you in the currency to which you've become accustomed."

Her dark eyes sparkle, and she stomps into the back room, still cackling under her breath.

When I enter the upstairs apartment, Grams has amassed an impressive pile of clothing on the antique bed.

"Isadora! I can't even fit all that in two suitcases! We seriously need to weed some of this out. I'm only going to be gone for a week."

"You have no idea what you might come across. It's always best to be prepared." She whooshes back into the closet for more.

I cautiously approach the mountain of couture as though there may be a scorpion lurking amongst the fabrics, and quickly sort the ball gowns, cocktail dresses, and four-inch heels into the "not on your life" pile. Now the stack is down to a manageable size.

Ghost-ma returns with an armload of athletic wear. "I almost forgot the yoga gear!"

"I wonder why?" We both chuckle, and I start folding and packing.

Pye enters from one of his hidden passageways and climbs directly into the suitcase.

"What in the world are you doing? You can't go to Arizona, Pyewacket!"

"R-oooow." Mournful cry.

"Don't worry, son, I got you. Silas is going to stay here with you, and Howie got everything set up. Let's test the system and make sure it's still caracal friendly. Does that sound good?"

"Reow." Can confirm.

Pyewacket reluctantly climbs out of my luggage and hops into the chair in front of the large computer screen.

I pull out my phone and call the number I have coded in my phone as "Headquarters."

A tune jingle-jangles from the speakers as an icon flashes on the screen.

Pyewacket taps the keyboard with one of his powerful paws to answer the call.

My image immediately springs to life on the screen and he rises on his hind legs with his two front feet on the desk.

On my screen, all I see are whiskers.

"Hey, buddy, you need to sink a little lower. So I can see your gorgeous face."

I swear to you, he groans as though I've made the world's lamest joke.

Lowering down to his forepaws, his majestic ears and wise golden eyes fill the screen.

"Now there's a face I could talk to for hours. Looks like we're all set for videoconferencing, Mr. Cuddlekins. And you know you have to stay out of Twiggy's way and take care of Grams. She'd be an absolute wreck without you."

As though the mere mention of her name can summon her like Beetlejuice, Ghost-ma pops out of the closet with three bathing suit options.

However, when she sees the videoconferencing system activated, her ability to hold physical objects vanishes, and everything drops to the floor. "Mitzy! I'm going to miss you terribly."

"It's only a week, Grams. Twiggy will be here. And Silas will be staying here to keep Pye out of trouble. And—"

"What about Odell? Maybe you can run down to the diner and make sure my handsome first husband will make at least one trip here?"

"Anything for you, Grams." Turning on my heels, I head for the door a bit too eagerly.

She floats next to me and arches one perfectly drawn brow. "I hope you're rushing to do my bidding because of your deep affection for me, and not your obsession with fries!"

"Guilty as charged." The bookcase door slides open, and my grandmother's tinkling laughter spills into the bookshop.

CUT TO —

Myrtle's Diner holds all the welcoming aromas of the delicious food my grandfather cooks.

I walk across the black-and-white-checked floor and slide into a booth.

Odell gives me a spatula salute through the red-Formica-trimmed orders-up window.

There's no splash of a basket of fries dropping into hot oil, but that's probably because he dropped it in a minute before I came through the door. It was shocking to discover Odell had his own set of clairvoyant abilities. Although, it shouldn't have been terribly surprising. With all of my gifts certainly coming from various branches of my family tree, when I uncovered the truth about Odell being my biological grandfather, his knack for knowing exactly what his regular customers needed without them having to order seemed logical and comforting.

The world's best waitress, Tally, sidles up next to my table, grinning broadly. Her tightly wound flame-red bun bobs its own greeting. "How are you doing, Mitzy? You want coffee or pop?"

"I'll definitely take a coffee, and keep 'em coming."

She laughs and shuffles off to fill my request. My grandfather quickly replaces Tally, bearing a plate of golden fried perfection.

Rather than place my order on the table and depart, he sets the plate in front of me as he slides onto the bench seat opposite.

"Did Myrtle Isadora send you?"

My mouth is too full for a reply, so I flash my eyebrows and nod.

The lines around Odell's eyes crinkle as he smiles with warm thoughts of my grandmother. "Yeah, I haven't had time to get over there for a visit in a couple of days. I know how she gets."

Washing down my fries with a slug of coffee, I wipe my mouth and launch into my pitch. "Erick and I are taking a case in Arizona. We'll be gone for about a week and, as you said, you know how she gets. She sent me down here to extract a promise that you'll check in on her. Will you do it?"

His coffee-brown eyes sparkle with mischief. "It would be my pleasure. I can never thank you enough for putting us back together. You really are the world's best granddaughter."

"Awww, shucks. It was the least I could do in exchange for free burgers and fries for life."

Odell grins, slides out of the booth, and wraps his knuckles twice on the silver-flecked white Formica tabletop before heading back to the kitchen.

CHAPTER 5

As I put the finishing touches on my packing duet back at the apartment, the bookcase door slides open and catches me off guard. I know how that must sound, but even psychics get surprised.

"Detective Harper. To what do I owe the pleasure?"

Before he can answer, I see the small case in his left hand.

"Wait, let me guess. You need me to put your gun in my checked bag."

"You know me so well, Schmoopie." He flutters a couple button-down shirts in my direction. "Can you throw these in your bag, too? They'll get wrinkled in my backpack."

Ignoring the shirts — which I can easily fit in my mammoth bag — I walk toward him, wagging my finger firmly. "Nope. We promised we weren't going to do foolish pet names, and I'm not gonna give up on that oath before we even hit our one-year anniversary."

He blushes adorably and shrugs. "Okay, but I can't keep calling you Moon for the rest of your life, can I?"

"Why not? It's my name, isn't it?" I cross my arms, tilt my chin up, and dare him to disagree.

He exhales, and his handsome face offers an obvious expression of surrender. "Whatever you say, dear."

"Touché." I take the small gun case from him and confirm that it is secured. Then I pack it between layers of couture in my largest suitcase.

"By the way, I booked a later flight than last time. Seems like you were dragging me out of here at some regrettably ungodly hour. Our flight doesn't leave until noon tomorrow, and we'll change planes in Chicago."

He nods. "I may not be the sheriff anymore, but my buddy at the airport will still make checking in and going through security a breeze. If we get there by 11:00 or so, we should be fine."

"Yeah, we should be. We're the only two people on the flight." I chuckle at the absolute smallness of our town, before uttering an exhausted sigh as I collapse onto the settee. "Do you feel like cooking tonight, or should I order takeout from that Chinese restaurant we like?"

"Hmmmm, I better cook. If we're going to be out of town for a week, there are a few things in the fridge we should use up."

I cross my arms and stick out my lower lip.

He shakes his head. "Guess what? If there are no pet names, then there's no pointless take out. We both get to have rules in the relationship, *Moon*."

Laying my head back against the soft cushion, I groan dramatically. "I can't believe I married such a grown-up. If I'm not careful, you'll have *me* cooking in no time."

He laughs heartily as he walks out of the apartment toward the three-story walk-up attached to the other side of the bookshop. "I might be talented, but I am no miracle worker."

As the secret bookcase door slides closed, I shout, "Rude!"

Not wanting to appear utterly helpless, I drag my large suitcases past the perfectly aligned oak reading desks with their brass lamps and green glass shades. However, I don't go so far as to lug them down the winding staircase.

As I head down solo, Pyewacket leaps from the bookcase where he was hiding and races past me. "Take it easy, son. You might knock me over."

"Reow." Can confirm.

Surprisingly, he waits for me at the bottom of the steps. When I reach him, he drops something in my path.

If I've learned anything since arriving in Pin Cherry Harbor, it's that my wise caracal is connected to a dimension beyond my understanding. When he offers me a gift, it's almost always an important clue. Crouching next to him, I scratch his broad tan head as I reach for the torn chunk of paper. "Well, Mr. Cuddlekins, what have you brought me?"

Scanning the old magazine article, I note the number of "open to the public" sweat lodges popping up across the country. This particular article makes no mention of the use of sacred land by non-natives, but it does clearly explain how lucrative the practice of pay-per-sweat has become.

"Thanks, Pyewacket. I'm with you. I already figured that we're going to uncover some kind of scam. Whether that will be connected to this missing woman or not remains to be seen. Although, if you're giving me this, it seems like you already suspect the connection. Right?"

"RE-OW!" Game on!

When I stand, the phone in my back pocket rings.

"Mr. Willoughby, are you headed into town?"

"Indeed. I have some items that may prove

useful on your journey. Are you and your husband dining out this evening or will I find you in the walk-up?"

"My practical and talented husband is making me dinner. He thought it would be wise to clear out the refrigerator before we headed out of town."

Silas chuckles, and I can easily picture him smoothing his bushy grey mustache with a thumb and forefinger. "That Mr. Harper is a real gem. I shall see you shortly."

"Sounds good." Ending the call, I walk between the stacks on the first floor and make my way toward the "Employees Only" door leading into the former printing museum. When I push the bar and the door creaks open, a lovely aroma greets me.

Pyewacket rockets past me, probably eager for scraps, and I inhale deeply as I join him. "I don't know what magic you've created in this kitchen, Harper, but it smells amazing."

He adjusts the flame of one of the burners on our six-burner gas, slide-in range, while I grab a seat opposite the stove and lean heavily on the polished granite countertop. "Does it bug you that I don't cook?"

He shrugs. "Not really. When I was taking care of my mother and she was staying with me at the old house, she did practically all the cooking. I've kind of always enjoyed it and, to be honest, I missed it. I'm not saying I'm going to be cooking you three squares a day for the rest of our lives, but it's a fun pastime right now."

"Maybe when we get back from Arizona, we can institute a cooking lesson Sunday or something like that."

His laughter is too easy and a little too loud. "Whatever you say, Moon. In between cases, we can definitely have some cooking lessons if you want. No pressure from my side."

He turns off the burner and plates the delicious dinner he created from things we needed to use up. Roasted asparagus, some delicious-looking burger patty, and home fries that might make Odell worry.

Erick carries the plates to the table, and I grab my precious Tabasco sauce from the fridge.

Turning, he slips his arms around my waist as I approach the table. "Hey, I was just heading back to grab that."

Rising on my tiptoes, I kiss his pouty mouth. "As usual, great minds think alike."

We sit down next to each other at the table, and I slather my golden home fries with Tabasco sauce. However, before I can pop a luscious beauty into my mouth, our doorbell rings and surprises the be-jeezus out of me.

My unflappable husband places a calming hand

on my shoulder. "It's only the new doorbell. I know it doesn't ring very often. I'll see who it is."

I'm pretty sure it's Silas, so I shove several bites of food in my mouth, chewing and swallowing as quickly as I can. Seems like my dinner is about to be interrupted, and I'm eager to eat as much of it as I can while it's still hot.

Silas shuffles in, and, to no one's surprise, is wearing his standard fusty old tweed coat, mystery stained shirt, and crooked bowtie.

Hastily wiping my mouth on a napkin, I throw back a gulp of water and get to my feet. "Silas. Thank you for bringing the stuff over. Am I right in assuming it will need an explanation?"

"You are correct. I shall take a seat in the living room and wait for you to join me."

Part of me wishes that was permission to finish my dinner, but the student inside me knows better. I immediately join my mentor on the leather sofa.

Erick returns to the table and continues to eat his dinner.

Jealous.

"I did some research on the tribes in that area. There are Navajo, Hopi, Yavapai-Apache, and long ago there was a tribe known as the Anasazi. Without knowing the specific location of the sweat lodge, I couldn't be certain which traditions and energies may reside in the land."

I'll hold my questions until I see what he's brought me.

"The first item is a simple regenerative tincture. If you must endure a sweat, or perhaps a vision quest, this green vial contains a liquid that will almost instantly restore your energy and focus."

This good-girl act can only last for so long. "Silas, you know you could make a fortune if you bottled this stuff commercially, right?"

He harrumphs, and his milky-blue eyes seem to penetrate my flesh. "There are more important things in life than money, Mizithra."

Yep, I should've kept my mouth shut.

"The second item is a dreamcatcher."

"Like the necklace my mom left me! I know what those are for. They're used to catch bad dreams and—"

He raises one commanding finger, and my vocal abilities vanish. "It is not that kind of dreamcatcher. I haven't much time, and it is important that you listen to the details of these tools."

I don't dare open my mouth. I simply nod.

"This dreamcatcher is a talisman. It has been imbued with recovery energy." Once again, he raises his finger before I can form a question. "Not recovery from exhaustion. Instead it will aid in recovery of a lost item. It may not be practical for you to use your pendulum and a map in Arizona. We don't know the circumstances of the case, or where you'll be staying. I chose the symbol of the dream-catcher because it would not draw attention. The energies that have been woven into the object are specifically designed to locate something that is lost. To recover said item or person. You may only use it once, and once you speak the name of the item or the name of the person, you will only have one hour until the energies dissipate. Use it wisely."

Once again, I press my lips together and nod silently.

He reaches into one of the many hidden pockets in his old coat. "The final item is a piece of jewelry. As I mentioned, it would not be safe for you to use the truth runes or the reversal symbols on sacred land. However, this necklace holds a stone known as hematite. The mineral has magnetic prop-erties and, when enhanced with alchemy, that phys-ical magnetism becomes psychological. In a sense, you will mesmerize your subject into telling you the unvarnished truth."

My eyes dart toward Erick, and Silas har-rumphs. "This is no parlor trick, Mizithra. This is a powerful item, and I will expect you to return it to me when you have finished your business in the Southwest. Over the years, you've proven trustwor-thy. I would not remove such an important artifact from my vault if I did not have faith in your ability to use it judiciously." He steeples his fingers and bounces his chin thoughtfully on the tips of his pointers.

This feels like the end of the lesson, and an opportunity for me to speak. Here goes nothing! "I appreciate you trusting me, Silas. I won't let you down. I have no idea what we'll find, but, like any case, I know there will be people who aren't being completely honest. I'm sure this will be very helpful. Thank you."

Despite Erick being within earshot of the entire exchange, he displays a level of self-control I can only dream of. Turning toward him, I have to ask, "Erick, what do you think about this?"

He finishes his last piece of asparagus, wipes his mouth, and smiles. "Like I always say, Moon, we play to our strengths. I'm bringing the firepower, and you're bringing whatever all that stuff is. I trust in your abilities — your hunches. Hopefully, we find this missing woman alive, but, if not, I'm confident that together we'll bring the perpetrator to justice."

That's my guy. I offer him a quick finger gun and smile at Silas.

"Can I get you anything to drink, Mr. Willoughby?"

He rises from the sofa and smiles warmly. "I

must be getting home. I shall return on the morrow, after your departure."

I know he'll grumble, but I can't help myself. I throw my arms around his neck and kiss his jowly cheek. "Thank you. I feel better knowing that you've given me these tools."

He whispers quietly. "Do not take unnecessary risks, Mitzy. I look forward to your return."

"Same. Oh, can you have a chat with Pye on your way out? Try to convince him to play nice with the workers until you get here tomorrow. All right?"

"Indeed."

With that he shuffles into the bookshop and closes the door behind himself, as I glance down at the items on the coffee table.

Erick joins me, kisses the top of my head, and whispers, "Harper and Moon are on the case."

CHAPTER 6
ERICK

"Mitzy, honey, you gotta wake up." I gently shake her shoulders and try to make waking up sound fun.

My bride is not a morning person, so if there was anyone else I could have tasked with waking her, I would have. That wily cat slunk away at the mere mention of it.

She pulls the sheet up over her adorable snow-white head and mumbles, "Just fifteen more minutes, Mom."

"Hey, Moon. They canceled our high-noon flight. Henry, over at the airport, arranged another pilot, but we gotta go now. The guy could only take a flight before 7:00 a.m."

Mitzy groans as though I've threatened to lock her in a cage with a wild bear as she continues her protest. "I hate airports! I hate planes! Travel is dumb!" She attempts to roll out of the bed, but I can see her feet tangling in the sheets.

Leaping to her aid, I catch her before she hits the floor.

"I've already loaded all the luggage into the Jeep, and there's a fresh pot of coffee waiting for you downstairs. All you need to do is trip and fall into some clothes, and we're outta here."

She drapes her lovely arms around my neck and attempts a new angle. "If you let me go back to bed, Detective Too-Hot-To-Handle, I'll make it worth your while."

Chuckling, I kiss her forehead and turn her toward the bathroom. "Save some of that energy for the first-class flight I'm sure you booked out of Chicago. If memory serves, they have a roomy sleeping pod on the Dreamliner 787."

Her beautiful grey eyes open wide, and her cheeks blush ruby-red. She loses no time in changing the subject. "Be ready in five minutes."

"That's what I thought." Pulling out my phone, I tap the timer and make the announcement. "And the clock is ticking, Moon!"

Some serious grumbling echoes from the marble-tiled bathroom as water splashes hither and yon.

My bride shuffles out of the bathroom and into the walk-in closet. It's not as glorious as the one she and her grandmother have kitted out in her old apartment on the other side of the bookshop, but it's bigger than any closet I've ever had.

It only takes her a minute to slip into skinny jeans and her comfortable canvas high-tops. However, when it comes to selecting a T-shirt, garments are flying like it's steak night in the chow hall.

She finally emerges in a cute red T-shirt with a sad coffee cup and a happy wineglass. The tagline reads, "Coffee, you're on the bench. Alcohol, you're up!"

"Seems like the perfect travel shirt, Moon. And good news, you made it." Stopping the timer on my phone, I slip an arm around her waist and lead her from our third-floor primary suite to the promised coffee on the first floor.

Pouring most of the pot into an extra-large travel mug, I add the appropriate amount of cream, secure the lid, and hand it to my near comatose wife as she walks out the front door.

Mitzy climbs into the passenger seat of the Jeep all by herself. I toss in her carry-on and carefully close the door.

When we arrive at the airport, the parking lot is unsurprisingly empty. Pin Cherry Harbor is famous for its shipping and rail lines. But we don't even have an official bus station; we're only a stop along the route. The official station is in Broken Rock.

The local airport mostly handles cargo planes, with the occasional inter-state hopper from larger metropolises down south, or, like today, a special charter flight.

Shouldering my backpack, I grab both of the large suitcases from the back of the Jeep and hope to high heaven that Mitzy will be ambulatory.

She steps out of the vehicle, places a fist on her sexy hip, and grins. "This is really good coffee, Harper. Is there anything you're not good at?"

The set up is too good to ignore. "I'm not that great at waking up my wife."

Mitzy spits her coffee in the parking lot, chokes, and pounds dramatically on her chest to catch her breath. "Touché, Harper. Touché."

Inside the terminal, I recognize most of the employees and offer a series of friendly waves and head nods.

We check our bags, and Henry gives me a quick reminder. "Don't forget, Mr. Harper, they may screen your checked bag at O'Hare Airport in Chicago. Listen carefully for your name over the PA. If they call you, get there on the double. Otherwise, they'll pull the firearm and send the bag through without it. Or, if they're feeling particularly nasty, they'll hold the entire bag and it won't make the flight."

"10-4, Henry. Thanks for the heads up."

Holding my backpack and Mitzy's small carry-on, we drop into a couple of chairs in the waiting area.

"Are you hungry? I could probably get to the diner and back before the flight takes off." I shrug and wait for her reply.

"You know what? I know this is going to sound shocking, but I'm actually not hungry. What's going on with me? Also, I remember how bumpy the flight was last time, from here to Chicago, and I don't want to put a bunch of food in my stomach only to see it make a return trip en route."

She cracks me up. We share a laugh, but she pulls out her phone.

"Am I boring you already, Moon?"

Mitzy blinks rapidly and shakes her head firmly. "No, no. I'm starting to wake up and only just realized I left without saying goodbye to Grams. She'll be upset, possibly furious."

Still learning to make sense of her ghostly grandmother, I inhale sharply. "We definitely don't want that. You should give her a call."

She scrunches up her mouth, tilts her head, and looks at me in frustration. "Yeah, that's what the phone is for."

"Withdrawn, Your Honor." I lean back and give her some space.

Mitzy laughs lightly and taps her phone.

This would be one of those instances where it's nice to live in a small town and be sitting in a practically empty airport.

Pyewacket's intense stare glares at us from the screen.

His mistress immediately attempts to placate him. "Hey, buddy. Twiggy will be there any minute to pour you a bowl full of your favorite children's cereal. Our flight got changed, and we had to leave in a hurry "

Mitzy suddenly stops speaking and seems to sit up straighter. The next thing I know, she's sputtering a series of excuses and defending the alcohol reference on her shirt. I can only assume staunch defender of Alcoholics Anonymous Isadora has joined Pyewacket on the phone call. I can't see the ghost or hear what the spirit might be saying, but the more time I spend at the bookshop surreptitiously studying Mitzy's reactions, the more I'm able to predict when Isadora enters a room.

"Isadora, if that's you, don't blame Mitzy for the sudden departure. I got a call early this morning from Henry at the airport. There was a snafu with our pilot, and our twelve o'clock flight got canceled. The best he could do was this 6:50 a.m. replacement. I had to throw everything in the car, including Mitzy, and it's absolutely all my fault that she didn't have time to say a proper goodbye."

Next to me, Mitzy rolls her eyes. "Oh gimme a break, Grams. When I tell you what happened, all I get to hear is how inconsiderate I am, but then Erick says basically the exact same thing, and suddenly he's a living saint!" She throws one arm in the air and jostles her phone.

Pyewacket mews in what I'm starting to believe is an angry tone.

Mitzy is on it in a minute. "Don't you start with me, son. I went out of my way to make sure Twiggy and Silas would be taking care of you, and frequently checking in on Grams. You'll be well looked after, and I'll be back in a week, so everyone needs to calm down. I haven't even finished my first cup of coffee!"

Without a single word of explanation, she hands me the phone and continues to nurse her giant mug of caffeine.

Staring at the cat staring at me, I shrug. "Hey, guy. You look great on camera."

"Reow." Can confirm.

That's about the only one of his sounds I can understand. "I hear you, buddy. I'll take good care of this one, and you watch out for Isadora. Between the two of us, we should be able to keep these gals safe for a week. What do you think?"

"RE-OW!"

He makes a strange vocalization that I don't understand, and I glance toward my wife.

"It's basically his version of 'game on.' It means that he's agreeing with you and accepting the challenge, or something like that."

We share some easy laughter. She takes her phone and ends the call.

"Hey, Henry is waving at us. Looks like it's time to board our flight. Are you ready for this, Moon?"

She leans against me and mumbles sleepily, "Harper and Moon, trying to wake up and get on the case."

I scoop an arm around her and hold her close as we head toward the tarmac. When I took the job as sheriff in the tiny town of Pin Cherry Harbor, I assumed all my big adventures were over. Then Mitzy Moon dropped into the middle of my life — it's been nothing but a colossal adventure ever since.

CHAPTER 7

THE DESCENT TO THE FLAGSTAFF airport is like flying inside a beautiful landscape painting. The Grand Canyon bisects the land, revealing colors more beautiful than I ever remember, and I promise myself I'll take Erick there after we solve the case.

The mountain air fills our senses when we step onto the tarmac.

Erick grins. "Wow! That sky is the clearest blue I've ever seen. Not a cloud in sight. Is that normal?"

Memories of endless days trying to eke out a living fade as I focus on the beauty surrounding us. "Totally. In the early afternoon the wind picks up and pushes gorgeous puffy clouds into the sky. In Sedona, it always looks like they're simply popping up from behind the red rocks. During monsoon season the clouds get dangerously grey and heavy, and the smell of pending rain is everywhere. It's one of the few sense memories I savor — from my transient barista days."

At the rental car counter, Mr. Harper is quick to request a Rubicon.

"We don't know what the roads will be like if we end up driving out to the land. I'd prefer something with some off-road capability if it comes to it."

"Copy that, Harper." Far be it from me to question his automotive decisions. My requirements are: starts when I turn the key; and doesn't have a clutch. Other than that, I can take it or leave it. Although, the gorgeous 1957 Mercedes 300SL silver coupe, with gullwing doors, that my grandmother left me is actually a thrill to drive. So there's that.

Erick waves his hand in front of my face and grins. "Don't check out just yet, Moon. I'm gonna need you to navigate."

"I'm here. You can count on me." I shift my weight impatiently from one foot to the other and clear my throat.

He grabs the keys from the counter and leads the way to our vehicle.

The lime-green metallic color definitely comes as a shock. I don't hate it, but all I'm saying is most rental cars are white, grey, or darker grey.

Erick loads our luggage, opens my door, and then hops into the driver's seat.

Rather than take Interstate 17, the main north-south artery, I guide him to the road less traveled — Highway 89A leading down Oak Creek Canyon.

"Wow! These roundabouts are new. Looks like time has been marching on in my absence." As I reflect on all that has happened, it's hard to believe three and a half years have slipped away since I escaped my life here.

Erick's easy manner shifts, and he grips the steering wheel firmly with both hands. "It's funny how that happens. Sometimes everything feels so connected, and you can't imagine how the universe could continue without you in it. Then you lose a loved one or friend and no one seems to miss a beat."

I know he's reliving something from his time in Afghanistan, but I'm hungry and possibly a little jet lagged. So I handle it the way I handle any uncomfortable emotion — with humor. "If you keep spouting wisdom like that, Harper, they're going to give *you* a job as a shaman in Sedona."

He chuckles, turns up the volume on the radio, and taps his thumb to the beat on the steering wheel.

As we approach the top of the switchbacks, I ask if he'd like to pull into the scenic overlook.

"No thanks. I prefer to drive through the

scenery. If I see something noteworthy, I'll stop for a photo."

"Sounds good to me."

We head into the tight turns on the back-and-forth road that quickly lowers us from a 7500-foot elevation to 5000 feet above sea level.

Driving down the canyon today feels different. I can almost imagine being a tourist in a town this stunning. Mountains reach toward the sky on either side of the two-lane road, and, as we twist and turn down the narrow canyon, we get peeks at the sparkling creek running alongside the road. There's a hint of fall color in the trees, and soon my favorite maples will display their red leaves and dot the landscape between the blackish-brown bark of the ponderosa pines.

"I don't think we drove up the canyon last time we were here, Moon. This is gorgeous. Did you spend a lot of time up here when you lived in Sedona?"

"Not exactly. I was kinda busy slinging coffee and occasionally paying my bills."

He hangs his head and exhales. "Remind me not to ask."

"Don't worry. Both my father and Silas made it eminently clear that I had a responsibility to clear any outstanding debts once I took possession of my inheritance. I'm not gonna get arrested and sent to debtor's prison, if that's what you're worried about."

"Debtor's prison? Did I just slip and fall into a Charles Dickens novel?"

"Nice one. That was a pretty sick burn, Harper." Changing gears, I attempt to bring it back to our mission. "We need to focus and make our plan. There's a fabulous hotel in the part of town locals call 'uptown.' I always dreamed of staying there. I had a short stint as a pizza delivery girl, and every time I had to take an order to that place, I would imagine what it must be like to stay in one of the private casitas."

"Sounds fancy. How many nights are we staying there?"

"Just one. We'll do our research and find a way to get on the land to look for Dean's gal. But that's future-me's problem. Tonight we stay at a schmancy hotel, dine in a fancy restaurant, and live it up while we can."

Erick points to the unique sign on our right. "Is that custom made?"

"Oh, you better believe it. Sedona can't have any old standard green-and-white city limits sign. An artistic sign with three dimensions is what they felt best welcomed tourists to their town."

We negotiate another new roundabout, and I give Erick directions to the hotel.

After booking a private casita next to the creek, we ask that our luggage be sent over.

The spectacular view of Oak Creek and the towering red rocks does not disappoint. I immediately open the French doors to enjoy the sound of the water burbling over the rocks.

Erick flops onto the massive bed and reaches for the remote.

"Hey, before you get too comfortable, Ricky, we should head into West Sedona and talk to Dean. We need to get the lowdown on the shaman. There's a chance we'll have to book ourselves a spiritual retreat."

He unbuttons his light-blue collared shirt and throws it on the bed.

No matter how many times I see those six-pack abs, one glance makes me forget how to speak.

He tracks my sight line, chuckles, and heads into the bathroom.

"Let me know when the suitcases get here."

"Copy that." I have no idea what he's doing. The shirt he was wearing seemed fine. But I'm not going to complain about him walking around our hotel room half dressed.

Before things can escalate, there's a light knock at the door, and they deliver my two large bags. Tipping generously, I thank the young woman who delivered them and close the door.

"The suitcases are here, Detective."

He walks out of the bathroom drying drips of water from his face. "Great. I'll put the gun in the safe, and then we can head over to Hot Kafka or whatever that coffee place is called now."

"Yeah, I can guarantee you it's called something else."

He locks up his weapon, puts on a fresh shirt, and grabs the car keys.

We take a brief detour to the creek before heading to the parking lot. He grins as he glances up and down the waterway. "Maybe we should get a cabin out here, Moon. I wouldn't mind visiting Sedona when we're not on a case."

"Let's not get ahead of ourselves, Harper. We'll solve this case, and then we'll see if you're still in love with Sedona after you've had more than a cursory glance about town."

"10-4, Moon."

"Actually, before we head over to the coffee shop, I'm going to make you a little bingo card, Harper." Returning to the room, I grab the notepad from the nightstand and draw a three square by three square bingo card. In each of the squares, I write a different word.

Passing the slip of paper to Erick, I give him instructions. "When we're in the coffee shop getting the skinny from Dean, you'll hear some, or, more likely, all of these words. You can keep track mentally or you can check off each box as it occurs."

Erick studies the paper for a moment and chuckles. "You expect Dean to say all of this?"

"In a perfect world, yes. But regardless of whether my former SUPERvisor fulfills that dream, there will be other tourists and locals lurking at surrounding tables. You *will* hear all of these words. That's a Mitzy Moon guarantee."

He holds the paper out as though preparing to read a proclamation. "Let me just run down the words and make sure I understand. Namaste. Vortex. Chakra. Aura Cleansing. I notice you put SUPER right in the middle to aid me in getting a tic-tac-toe."

"Hey, it's bingo, not tic-tac-toe. But, yeah. I know beyond a shadow of doubt we're going to hear that one!"

Erick continues. "Colonic." He puts his other hand over his mouth, scoffs uncomfortably, and arches an eyebrow.

"Hey, I don't make the rules. I'm just telling you about the game."

He shakes his head. "And now for our final row of words. Spiritual journey. Mother Earth. Blessing."

Taking a small bow, I lead the way to the rental car and open his door.

He climbs into the driver's seat, leans out, and kisses me square on the mouth. "Never let it be said Mitzy Moon is ordinary. I'm not talking about your special senses, Moon. I'm talking about the way you can make anything an adventure."

"You're not wrong."

Walking to the passenger side, I climb in and shout, "Hit it!"

CHAPTER 8

As we wend our way up to the main road, I can no longer keep flashes of my sketchy old life at bay. Not for the first time, I'm incredibly grateful Silas Willoughby found me.

Erick pulls onto Highway 89A, and I give directions to whatever the heck the Hot Kafka, which briefly became Crow's Coffee, is called now. I also remind him how businesses open and close faster than the doors on a cuckoo clock in this town. Apparently, there's not a great deal of "running of the numbers" prior to the launching of businesses.

"Makes sense, Moon. I'll be prepared."

However, when we pull into the parking lot, both of our mouths hang open for a moment.

I'm the first to regain my powers of speech.

"Brewed Dog — a Pet and Partner Café." I widen my eyes and shrug as I glance at Erick.

He tilts his head to the side and gives a nod reminiscent of Robert De Niro in *Raging Bull*. "Different strokes for different folks, they say."

We exit the vehicle and head into . . . heaven knows what.

As we enter the coffee shop, it appears that the predominant species of pet featured is dogs. There is one patchouli-anointed man with dishwater-blond dreadlocks seated at a high top in the corner. He's tapping away with focused intensity on his small laptop, while a large red-blue-and-green macaw perches on his left shoulder.

I smile, and squeal inwardly. Yup, I'm definitely in Sedona!

Erick catches my eye, and we proceed to the counter.

Before we have a chance to place an order, or even peruse the menu, an all-too-familiar voice calls out. "Mitzy! It's super great to see you! So glad you could make it happen."

My hubby mouths "Center square" and grins as he falls in line beside me.

Dean strides out from behind the counter in loose, drawstring, tie-dye pants and a T-shirt bearing the company logo — an owner and their dog sharing a latte.

"Dean, I'm sure you remember Erick Harper."

Erick reaches out for a handshake, but Dean hugs him instead. "Welcome, fellow soul."

Time to bail out my husband. "Hey, Dean, is there somewhere we can speak in private?"

He presses his hands together in prayer pose and offers a little bow. "Namaste."

Beside me, Erick whispers for my ears only. "Check."

It's all I can do to suppress a fit of giggles. "Good to see you, too. Can we talk in the back?"

"My new assistant manager is having an aura cleansing in the back right now. She had a blockage in her throat chakra, and we thought it best to handle it immediately."

"Of course. Good idea." Behind me I hear two more whispers of, "Check. Check." I surreptitiously attempt to elbow my husband and shut him up, but he easily dodges my weak maneuver. "How about out front?"

Dean opens his arms as though he's embracing the entirety of his clientele. "I have no secrets from these fellow travelers. We're all on a spiritual journey together. Why don't you two take a load off in those beanbags in the corner, and I'll make you a super cup of coffee, righty-o? Iced or hot?"

Erick is the first to answer. "I'll take mine hot, Dean."

Taking a deep breath and doing my best to hold it together, I put in my order. "I'll take mine iced. Thank you."

He makes a quick bow and ducks behind the counter.

Erick mumbles in my left ear, "Please tell me we're not sitting on beanbags."

"Wish granted." I lead the way to a table surrounded by three plush chairs.

It's not the height of privacy, but it's apparently the best we're going to get today.

Dean joins us with two iced beverages, and Erick's absolutely enormous hot beverage. My eyes nearly pop out of my head when I see the size of the cup, or, possibly, bowl. All I can picture is the opening sequence from *So I Married an Ax Murderer*. It takes a moment to shake that hilarious vision from my head.

"Mitzy Moon. I can't believe you're back in Sedona. Just super to see you!" Dean grins, adjusts his sun-bleached man-bun/topknot, and enjoys a hearty sip of his iced coffee.

"It's even more beautiful than I remember. I'm sorry for the circumstances that brought me out here, but I appreciated the phone call."

Dean tugs at his scruffy goatee and nods as though I've spoken the deepest proverb. "Be sure to get out and visit at least one vortex while you're here. Businesses change, new roads are created, but Mother Earth remains the same."

Erick reaches out and slips an arm around my shoulder. As he slides along my shoulders, he draws a little checkmark in the middle of my back. He's working harder to break me than Will Ferrell in a *Saturday Night Live* sketch.

"Can you tell us a little about what your girlfriend was doing the last time you spoke?"

Dean strokes his goatee twice, nods once, and responds. "She's healing from some intense trauma. Used to be in some kind of cult. She's totally working on cleansing her entire system. She's doing meditation, juice cleanses, yoga, and colonics."

Erick makes another checkmark on my back as he withdraws his arm.

"This sweat lodge experience was meant to be an attempt to purify her spirit. Shaman Kyle has been working in and around the Verde Valley for a couple of years now, and has many disciples. He recently opened the retreat center and folks are super pleased."

"Does Shaman Kyle own the property that he uses for these sweat lodges?"

"No. He created a spiritual contract with the Yavapai-Apache nation to set up a more permanent center. He uses their land in exchange for keeping the traditions alive. It's a symbiotic relationship."

7747

I feel as though I've thrown up a bit in my mouth. But I hold it together. "And how did your girlfriend—"

"Luminous Being. It's her legal name. I'm sure you've probably forgotten all the amazing spiritual aspects of this town, Mitzy, but finding your true self is definitely one of them. Finding your soul name is an added blessing."

Erick mouths, "Bingo!"

Oh brother. "How did Luminous hear about Shaman Kyle's sweat lodges?"

"Oh, he has a user-friendly website. I'll text you the link."

And so he does. Immediately.

"Thanks. I'll take a look at that later. How many days was she scheduled to be on the land?"

"She purchased the Solo Seeker Package with an optional Exclusivity upgrade. She didn't plan to avoid the other sojourners, but she wanted the option in case she encountered negative energy."

I can't be sure if it's out loud or not, but I sense an intense snicker of mirth from my partner.

"Did you have a question for Dean, Mr. Harper?" I attempt to stare daggers at Erick. He deflects them without lifting a finger.

"Just one. Does Shaman Kyle have a license to conduct these sweat lodges? Or possibly the proper permits?"

Dean smiles and tilts his head as though he's explaining to a child why he or she can only have one cookie. "I completely understand where you're coming from, man. You're trapped in the rat race of rules and regulations. It's hard to embrace a free spirit like Shaman Kyle's. He received a blessing from the tribal elders and that's all the permission he needs. There are no permits required on tribal land."

Erick inhales sharply, and I swear I hear him mumble, "Convenient."

I pick up the baton and ask my next question. "I'm sorry to have to ask this, Dean. Were you and Luminous having any problems — in your relationship — before she left for this retreat?"

He places his hands together in prayer pose once again and bows. "A fair question, Mitzy. Our relationship is solid. I've been very supportive of her transition from mindless acolyte to a more spiritual path. There have been some bumps along the way, but we always keep the channels of communication open between us and Mother Earth."

"All right. Does she have any other family or close friends in the area?"

He smiles warmly, but I sense him withdraw. "We consciously chose not to drag any baggage into this new energetic bond. Neither of us has had the opportunity, or desire, to unpack our pasts.

I know she fled the cult in New Mexico, but I never pushed her for details. We're about focusing our energy on building a more harmonious future."

"Understood. Just wondering if there's anyone she may have gone to visit, if she had a reason to leave the land early."

"Oh, she belongs to a hot yoga group, and she generally takes part in the full-moon drum circle up on Cathedral Rock. Other than that, she's super new in town and hasn't made a ton of friends. She's more withdrawn. I'm kind of the social core of the relationship." Dean laughs too easily.

"Got it."

Glancing at Erick, I find myself fresh out of questions.

My husband leans forward and stares directly at Dean. "I believe you told Mitzy you drove out to the land, to look for Luminous Being. Were you able to speak directly to Shaman Kyle on that visit?"

Dean fidgets uncomfortably in his chair. "Hey, man, you'll have to excuse my exaggeration. I may have been syncing with a dark vibration that day."

My extra senses instantly click into high. "What do you mean?"

"I did drive out to the land. But I wasn't allowed past the gates. You have to have a reservation or a private invitation from Shaman Kyle. I totally connected with the man in the guard shack. I described her vehicle, and—"

Putting up my hands, I motion for him to stop. "Hold on, Dean. When we talked on the phone, you said you'd spoken to some of the other people at the retreat. You said they specifically told you she'd left early. Were you lying to me?"

He presses his hands together in prayer pose and leans forward. "Sorry. Super sorry. I kind of combined two different things. I did drive out there, but the couple I spoke to was here in the coffee shop. They recognized my girlfriend's picture." He points to a painting hanging behind the bar.

Erick twists in his chair, and we gasp simultaneously.

The intensely bright acrylic painting is a somewhat abstract nude painted entirely with a palette knife. The face is fairly identifiable, but there are other assets featured more prominently.

Dean clears his throat and attempts to win us back. "It was her face they recognized. And they said her tiny blonde braids were unmistakable." His heart is racing.

"Look, Dean. Do I wish you had been more honest with me? Yes. Am I still going to look into the disappearance of Luminous Being? Yes. But moving forward, no more lies. You're not helping anyone by withholding information from us."

Dean hangs his head like a scolded puppy. "You got it, Mitzy. Again, I'm super sorry."

Erick gets up from his chair, offers his hand to Dean, and when Dean shakes it, Erick grips it tightly. "Dean, if you weren't a friend of Mitzy's, I'd be driving her back to the airport right now. Mitzy and I don't appreciate being brought out here under false pretenses. If it turns out you and your girl-friend are having some kind of disagreement and she simply drove away from this retreat to hang out with a girlfriend, we'll be having another chat."

Dean rockets to his feet, standing head and shoulders below Erick, and nods furiously. "Under-stood. I super appreciate you guys looking into this. Seriously, super appreciate it."

Erick nods curtly and escorts me from the Brewed Dog Café.

CHAPTER 9

ON THE WAY BACK to our upscale hotel, I quiz Erick. "Hey, why did you yank us out of there so fast?"

He exhales and drags his left thumb along his stubbled jaw. "I felt it was my husbandly duty to be indignant for you. Really bugs me that this guy baited you into coming out here with half-truths."

"Fair enough. It kind of bugged me too, but I'm so used to suspects lying in these situations, I honestly wasn't surprised."

Erick presses both hands against the steering wheel, leans back and glances sideways. "Hold on. You're telling me you think Dean might be responsible for his girlfriend's disappearance?"

"A handsome sheriff once told me that everyone is a suspect until they're not." I smirk and blow him a kiss.

"Wow, I guess that calls for a 'touché,' eh, Moon?"

We chuckle, and he pulls up to the valet stand.

"Look at you, Detective. Getting all fancy and stuff with valet parking."

He grins. "You said tonight we were living large. Fancy hotel, expensive dinner, possible second honeymoon—"

My eyes stretch to their widest, but any snarky retort is prevented when the valet opens my door and offers me his hand.

I don't take it, because sometimes I get weird psychic flashes when I touch people. Don't worry, I'm nice about it. "Thanks. I got it."

He moves to the opposite side of the vehicle, accepts the keys, and gives Erick a pick-up ticket.

Heading back to the room, Erick asks if he should change for dinner.

Stifling my scoff, I patiently reply. "Look, Sedona may have hotels and restaurants with hefty price tags, but that's only because tourists will pay. It's actually not a fancy town. You'd be hard-pressed to find anyone, even a legit business person, wearing a tie."

He smiles. "Understood. You better call your grandmother and that— What do you call him? Demon spawn?"

The color temporarily drains from my face.

"Oh, my gosh! I should've called them as soon as we landed. On it!"

I tap the speed dial for Headquarters, and a moment later the whiskered judgment of my furry overlord fills my screen.

"Heeeeey, Pyewacket. How's my favorite fur baby? I miss you like crazy."

Silence. His gleaming golden eyes weigh me and find me wanting.

In a flash Ghost-ma shoves in behind him and voices her disappointment. "Mitzy! You were supposed to land hours ago. We've been worried sick. You know how often planes crash."

"Let's dial it back twenty to twenty-five percent, Isadora. Actually, planes don't crash that often, and I'm beginning to think you simply enjoy worrying."

Behind me, Erick snickers into his hand.

"Well, Mr. Cuddlekins and I were worried sick. We've been afraid to leave the apartment in case we missed a call."

"And how does this differ from your usual daily schedule? Let's see, Pyewacket's consists of: wake up Mitzy; demand Fruity Puffs; nap all day. And yours . . . Remind me."

"Well, I never!" She crosses her bejeweled arms and lifts her proud chin.

Pyewacket makes a sound reminiscent of a human scoff.

"You know what, Myrtle Isadora? I think we both know that's not true. I'll spare you the litany of last names . . . But I'm thinking it. Can you read my thoughts long distance?"

The expression on her face shifts, and the glow drains from her apparition like a fading sunset.

"No! Oh dear. I absolutely can't. Are you holding your mind blank like Silas taught you?"

"No. Actually, I was thinking about how much I miss you guys. But I'm happy to know that distance creates its own barrier."

"Mitzy! That's a terrible thing to say." Her glow returns with her ire.

"We can discuss the finer points of privacy when I get home, Grams. I made the call to bring you and Pyewacket up to speed on what we know so far. Erick's on line perusing Shaman Kyle's website so we can purchase a package and have a cover story for going on the land."

Pyewacket covers his eyes with one paw, and Grams laughs until ectoplasm leaks from her ethereal nose. "Did you say 'Shaman Kyle'? Oh dear! If I didn't know better, I'd say he's definitely guilty of something."

"He's absolutely guilty of bad taste, Grams. We won't know anything for sure until Erick and I get out there and do some more investigating. But you can get started on the murder board." I give her the remaining details on our meeting with Dean and the discovery of his dishonesty.

"That's an abuse of friendship. I hope you told him as much."

"No, I didn't, but Erick gave him a warning handshake and swept me out of there as though I was the president in *White House Down*."

Grams nods her approval. "You tell him I'm very proud. That's exactly the correct response."

Glancing toward our small living room, I see that Erick is once again shirtless. I lose my entire train of thought, and my jaw simply hangs like a broken wind chime on a still day.

"Sweetie? What's the matter? Did this freeze or lag, or whatever you call it?"

I regain composure, swallow, and pass along her message.

Erick looks as though he's about to rise from the couch, and I simply cannot have all of that on screen.

"He says thanks, Grams. We've got to end the call, anyway." Turning back to my screen, I lean in to fill the camera lens and wave too cheerily. "All right, we're about to go to dinner. I'll update you guys tomorrow. Love you."

Ghost-ma arches one perfectly drawn brow and snickers wickedly. "Message received, Mizithra."

Blerg.

Ending the call, I turn to admonish my careless husband for his lack of apparel, but he beats me to the punch with a soft embrace and a welcome kiss.

"So, where are we going to dinner, Moon?"

Ignoring the flush on my cheeks, I proceed. "There's a place not far from here that has an absolutely amazing view. It was completely out of my price range when I lived in town, but I think Mitzy Moon, courtesy of Myrtle Isadora, could swing a lovely meal there now. How does that sound?"

He pulls me closer and his eyes turn into that smoky, dreamy trap I call "Ricky Quicksand." Of course, that's only in my mind. I'd never give him the satisfaction of saying it out loud.

"How would you feel about room service, Moon?"

Struggling to extract myself from his carefully constructed web, I giggle foolishly. "Ricky! We almost never come here. It would be a shame not to enjoy the view for at least one night. We have no idea where the land is. It might be gorgeous there or it might be tucked into a kind of crappy place. I hate to say it, but our government didn't exactly select the choicest sections of land for the Native American reservations."

Erick nods in agreement. "True. Let's go out for supper, and I can tell you what I found out about Shaman Kyle's spiritual-awakening packages."

My eyes roll so hard I fear I may pop an ocular tendon, and my response drips with sarcasm. "Can't wait. I mean, for the intel. Supper will be divine."

He re-dons on his carefully preserved fitted button-down, short-sleeved shirt, and I acquiesce to the voice of Grams in my head and pop into a sundress. It's actually not half bad.

The valet retrieves our car, and Erick drives one-handed as he holds my hand in his, all the way into the lobby of Libélula.

The view is spectacular, and signs of a late monsoon storm rise over the mountains. The fully covered alfresco dining area protects us from the weather while allowing us to enjoy the glorious dark clouds and brilliant strikes of lightning as the storm rolls toward us. Each drop of water sweetens the air with moisture, and I inhale the familiar scent of creosote bushes accepting the desert's gift of rain.

Dining on a variety of unique and exotic tapas, such as gambas espinaca, romesco bruschetta, beef pinchos, and goat-cheese-stuffed figs, we wile away several hours and a bottle of outrageously expensive wine.

The storm's cracks of thunder grow quieter as it passes over us and continues its route southeast while we prepare our plan for tomorrow.

Erick shares his findings on Shaman Kyle's website. "They have more than nine packages. But I thought it would be best to invest in a couples' package that extends the various experiences over four days. We can always leave sooner, but that will give us time to inspect the grounds, chat with the other guests, and hopefully find Luminous Being."

"Yeah. That sounds good. What does the couples' package include?"

Erick flicks through a couple of screens on his phone and reads directly from the site. "A welcoming drum circle will be provided to assist you in setting your intention. Then you may select an aura cleansing or a vision quest meditation, followed by a vortex bath. Your spiritual journey experience can be combined with a communication from your ancestors." At this point, he looks up at me and flashes his eyebrows. "Maybe you can give Shaman Kyle a little taste of his own medicine on that one."

We share a chuckle, and he continues.

"And then there's a variety of sweat lodge experiences to choose from. The advanced option includes four sweats in one day, which sounds like more than I can handle."

I down my last sip of wine and sigh. "Yeah, I think one trip through the hot, steamy hut is enough for me."

He tilts his head from side to side. "That's not really an option. The most basic package is the initiate level, and even that involves one sweat per day for four days. We'll probably have to purchase that one, and then maybe we can make excuses to skip days two through four."

Leaning forward, I walk my fingers across the table and turn my palm up. Erick places his hand in mine and smiles. I squeeze it and grin. "Leave the excuses to me, mister. I'm definitely next level in that department."

He laughs and rubs my hand. "True. Shaman Kyle won't know what hit him."

Back at our swanky casita, we pull our deck chairs out from under the overhang and gaze at the star-filled sky. As the waxing gibbous moon travels overhead, Erick takes my hand and whispers, "Isn't it about time for honeymoon, Take 2?"

Giggling, I lead the way into the casita.

Fade to black.

CHAPTER 10

A SOFT KNOCK ON OUR DOOR signals the arrival of the much-anticipated morning room service.

I hide under the covers, while my more mature and far more prepared husband answers the door, allows them to set our table, and tips them generously.

As soon as the hotel staff leaves, I pop out from under the covers and descend on the full breakfast spread. There's a basket of chocolate croissants, a carafe of orange juice, a large pot of coffee, tiny pitchers of cream so cold there's condensation on the outside, and the pièce de résistance — scrambled eggs with chorizo, golden home fries, and a miniature bottle of Tabasco.

"Knocked it outta the park, Harper. This is like a breakfast from one of my favorite dreams."

He pulls me into his arms and smiles. "Are you telling me your favorite dreams are about breakfast food and not me?"

Glancing down, I whisper, "I dream about you, too."

Shaking his head, he laughs as he takes his seat in front of a stack of fluffy pancakes.

We make quick work of breakfast before packing our bags.

Erick calls up a map on his phone, flicks to the turn-by-turn directions, and takes a screenshot.

"Why a screenshot?" I lean in and stare at the image on his phone.

"We don't know what the signal will be like on the way to the land. I don't want to get lost on the way to our big case."

Lifting both of my hands in the air, I smile. "No judgment, Harper. I just like watching you work."

Rather than waste time waiting for someone to come and collect our bags, Erick transports everything to the valet stand and they quickly retrieve our car.

As he navigates the route to Shaman Kyle's spiritual retreat center, familiar signs and sights grab my attention.

"Oh, looks like we're headed toward Camp Verde. Interesting that Shaman Kyle advertises his retreat center as being in Sedona. That seems like more of a marketing tactic than a truism."

My husband shrugs. "I'll take your word for it, Moon. I'm just following the directions. I have no idea where Sedona ends and this Camp whatever begins."

Eventually, we turn onto a narrow, Forest Service dirt road that is badly in need of grading.

"Yeesh! I hope I don't lose my breakfast."

My concerned driver reaches across and rubs my knee. "Aren't you glad I got the four-wheel drive, though?"

"Don't break your arm patting yourself on the back, Ricky. Maybe slow down a little so I don't up-chuck in your brilliant rental."

Erick kindly slows the pace for me and, after two more miles of bumps, potholes, and two sudden stops for bolting jackrabbits, the infamous guard shack looms into view.

Coming to a complete stop, Erick lowers his window. "Good morning. We're checking in for our retreat."

The teenager in the booth is barely interested. "Name?"

Reaching across, I poke Erick in the side. He swats my hand away and attempts to keep his composure. "Erick Harper and Mitzy Moon."

The messy-haired teen doesn't even look up

from his clipboard. He hands us a parking pass and mumbles, "You have to hang this from your rearview mirror. Follow the signs." With that, he returns to his previous slouch and taps away at the screen on his phone.

"Wow! I'm having a hard time believing Dean had a meaningful conversation with *that*. Let's hope Shaman Kyle is better versed in customer service than that punk."

Erick chuckles. "Think back to the jobs we held at that age, Moon." He arches one eyebrow and returns his attention to the road ahead.

Before long we arrive. He turns off the engine, shoves the keys in his pocket, and grips my hand. "I don't know if I'm ready for this, Moon."

"Stick with me, Harper. I'll make sure no one cleanses your aura without your permission."

As we hop out of the vehicle, a young woman in a gauzy tie-dye sundress flits toward us.

"Welcome to the land. I'm Desert Flower. Shaman Kyle is expecting you." She hugs us each in turn, not asking for permission.

Our arrival on "the land" is a completely different experience than the guard booth.

"Will we be seeing Shaman Kyle today?" My voice goes up at the end, and my doubt seems clear. However, all of that escapes our blessed host.

"Of course. Shaman Kyle welcomes each of his

sojourners personally. I'll get you checked in and show you to your yurt." She closes her eyes, seeming to savor the experience of saying his name.

At the mention of a yurt, my heart skips a beat. Not in a good way. I'm not a fan of camping, so the thought of spending a week in an octagonal tent-like structure with a pressboard floor does not excite.

She shows us to a pair of sky chairs hanging from the branches of a large cottonwood tree. I recognize the design from the Ren Faire back in Pin Cherry Harbor where I once went under cover selling pickles, but that's another story.

After handing us each a clipboard, she proceeds with her careful instructions. "The first page is strictly informational. Read and sign. Page two requires a bit of personal information, for your safety and well being while on the land. Page three may be filled out now, or after the drum circle. You may receive clarification on your intentions and outcomes once you have truly settled into the spirit of this place."

Keeping my opinions to myself, I scan page one, fill in the bare minimum of information on page two, and scratch out a hasty "cleanse my auras and recharge my creativity" intention on page three.

When I glance toward my partner, he seems to be taking things far more seriously.

Fortunately, he looks up, and I attempt to send him a silent *hustle it up* message. Maybe he gets it, or maybe he's simply done. Either way, we hand our clipboards back to Desert Flower.

She places them inside a small pop-up trailer a few feet behind her. When she returns, she motions for us to follow. "Let me take you to your yurt."

There's that word again.

We follow her to a disconcertingly small octagonal structure. The sides are canvas, the door zips open and closed, and the oilcloth roof may or may not keep out the weather.

The sooner we solve this case, the better.

"I'll allow you to settle in and find your balance. There will be a light meal this evening, and the drum circle begins at sunset."

As I look around the ten-foot diameter yurt, I can't imagine what I will do with myself between now and my light supper.

Erick, however, is miles ahead. "Is there a pond or creek on the land? We were hoping to explore nature a bit before supper."

You would think he offered her a doughnut. She smiles broadly and nods her head. "I'm so glad you asked, Mr. Harper. We passed by the open eating area and took a left after the first sweat lodge. We're in the residence area now. If you continue past the last yurt in the row, you will find your way to Beaver Creek. We had exceptionally high precipitation this winter, so the water is deep and fast flowing. If you're not a good swimmer, I wouldn't recommend entering the water."

He smiles and dips his head in that way that insinuates he's doffing a cap. "Thank you. I'm a strong swimmer. But today is only about exploration, no diving."

She laughs, bows slightly, and takes her leave.

Erick walks in a tiny circle at the center of our dwelling. "For the prices they charge, I would've thought there'd be more."

Sinking onto the mattress, which is directly on the floor, I groan. "I'm not exactly a 'roughing it' girl anymore. I had enough uncomfortable beds and cold showers to last a lifetime before Silas found me."

"Not too many beds, I hope." He laughs too easily.

Rather than a verbal retort, I stick out my tongue and wave my "finger antlers" at him.

Erick takes it in stride. "I'll grab the suitcases. Why don't you poke around the open eating area and see if you can make any friends?"

"Copy that."

He disappears out our front door flap, and I begrudgingly follow.

As I survey the open eating area, there's no joy

to be had. If there are any other *sojourners* on the land, they are otherwise occupied.

When he returns with the suitcases, I follow him into the yurt.

Erick carefully slips his gun case between a gap in the inner felt layer and the outer canvas layer, near the door.

As for the rest of our belongings, there's no place better than the suitcases they came in.

Following the simple directions to adventure — provided by Desert Flower — we arrive at Beaver Creek and discover four people frolicking in the cold water.

Erick grips my hand, squeezes it, and plasters on a huge grin. "Time to make friends, Moon."

Here goes nothin'.

My confident ex-lawman waves and walks to the edge of the rushing water. "Hey there! Erick and Mitzy over here. We're looking forward to getting to know everyone."

From my vantage point behind Erick's broad shoulders, I peer at the humans and offer a hesitant wave.

The two men closest to the shore wade over.

The tall, lithe blond flicks his hair out of his face and points to the shorter, pudgier bald guy on his left. "Welcome. I'm Winter and this is Ivan.

We've been soul-bonded for two years. This retreat is a reconnection exercise for us."

Erick accepts a damp hug from Winter. "Great to meet both of you. Mitzy and I are newlyweds. We're—"

My inner psychic feels he's reached the end of his woo woo vocabulary, and I step in. "We're cleansing our energy fields of old relationship baggage and hoping to connect with the wisdom of our ancestors." Winter makes no attempt to hug me. Instead, he presses his hands together in prayer pose and bows.

Ivan avoids eye contact and gestures to the water. "The water is great. You can pick your way across those rocks and sit on the—"

Winter interrupts. "I'm sure they know how to walk across a creek, Ivan. You're always telling everyone what to do. Let them be, Lamb."

Ivan nods and looks down. "What happened to your vow of silence?"

His partner scowls. "Hush. That's only around Shaman Kyle."

The remaining two attendees wave from their spot across the creek, but make no effort to come and introduce themselves.

Winter rolls his eyes and exhales. "That's Desiree and Jonathan. They're consciously coupled and they spend every breathing moment together.

Like, e-v-e-r-y moment." He grabs his shirt from a nearby tree limb and calls to Ivan. "Come on, Lamb. We have to meditate before supper."

Ivan smiles shyly, nods, and hurries after Winter.

Erick glances from the couple across the creek to the exiting pair, and grips both my hands. "We're in it now, Moon."

"Copy that."

CHAPTER 11

WHAT SOME APPARENTLY DESCRIBE AS a light supper, I describe as a snack for breath-airians! If you're not familiar with the term, it's one I heard frequently during my days in Sedona. A breath-airian is someone so in tune with the spiritual energies of the world they need neither food nor water to survive. They simply inhale the beauty of nature, and that alone sustains them.

As you know, I'm a french fries and burgers kinda girl. So, when Desert Flower calls us to supper and I discover a bowl of kale chips, an array of lettuces, radish slices, and celery shavings, I'm less than impressed.

But the kicker comes after our so-called meal.

Desert Flower holds a small woven basket in her hands and stands before the group.

"Mitzy and Erick, we are so pleased that you are joining this spiritual journey. I'll ask that you place your cell phones in the basket. We will secure them until you've finished your quest."

Erick looks at me, and I shrug.

A girl who wasn't among those we saw at the creek adds her two cents. "Everyone has to turn in their phones. It's part of disconnecting from the negative energies of the outside world."

Desert Flower encourages the peer pressure. "Thank you, Rheegan. As a nomad and a solo seeker, your contributions to the community are so important."

Pulling my phone from my back pocket, I toss it in the basket.

Erick seems more hesitant than I would've imagined, but eventually lays his own gently on top of mine.

Desert Flower utters a hearty. "Aho."

Leaning toward my hubby, I whisper, "That kinda means 'thank you' or 'I agree.'"

He chuckles.

Our hostess turns and heads toward the pop-up camper that Erick and I have decided must be the headquarters of their operation.

Erick hops up and follows.

Our hostess stops. "You can return to the circle, Erick."

"No problem. I'm sure you're going to lock my phone up tight. But I want to double check that the security is — secure."

Desert Flower's frustration emanates off her like a lighthouse beacon — to me, at least. She allows Erick to accompany her into the trailer, and they both return about a minute later.

Erick gives me an eyebrow arch and my psychic senses fill in the unspoken message: *We'll talk later.*

Two Trees introduces himself, sits cross-legged near the central fire, and thumps out a beat on his circular-frame drum. He holds the padded mallet loosely, shakes his mousy-brown dreadlocks, and closes his bloodshot eyes as he finds his rhythm.

The tempo rolls on and, for the first time since our arrival, Shaman Kyle appears. Fortunately, his cultural appropriation has its limits. He simply wears a tie-dyed T-shirt and some old-school board shorts. His wild brown curls are loosely tied back with a leather thong.

The shaman stretches his arms wide, intones a long howling hum, and begins his speech. "Over the next few days, you will journey toward your breaking point. When you reach this, only then can you truly rebuild your higher self. You will endure physical trials, meant to assist you in speaking to your spirit guides and better understanding the celestial information they carry. You came to this retreat for different reasons, but you all seek a new beginning. A cleansing of the past. A rebirth. Mother Earth shall take you into her womb, and from the spirit world you shall re-emerge with a new purpose."

Kyle produces a wooden flute and accompanies Two Trees in the unfamiliar song.

Desert Flower hands each participant a flat, circular drum and a mallet. "Let the spirit guide you. Join the rhythm when you feel led and share whatever beat comes to your heart."

Erick looks like he knows how to handle a drum. A childlike glee sparkles in his eyes as the firelight dances before us. I can imagine him as a boy, with a pint-sized drum. However, thanks to my extrasensory abilities, that imagining turns into a full-on clairvoyant vision. I clearly see Erick on one of those legendary camping trips with Odell and Nimkii. There's a glowing fire, a large Dutch oven with amazing aromas wafting from beneath its heavy lid, and Nimkii is teaching Erick how to drum.

"How sweet."

The drumming beside me ceases. Erick leans in. "What's sweet?"

Oops. "Didn't mean to say it out loud. Tell you later."

Shaman Kyle lets his flute drop to his lap. "It is

best if you remain silent during drumming circle. Words and images may come to you, but they are for you alone. There will be time to share when we begin to set the intentions."

Ouch! Shaman Kyle reminds me of every principal I ever disappointed at the many schools I visited during my unhappy years in foster care.

Focusing my attention on drumming, I refuse to let myself drift into another vision. I mean, I truly try.

The moody mood ring on my left hand heats to the point where it can no longer be ignored. Glancing down, I see the fierce gleaming eyes of Pyewacket staring straight through me. Gulp. I think we all know what that means.

For now, that message must remain unanswered.

Throwing myself into the drumming, I listen as Kyle asks around the circle, confirming each sojourner's intention.

Rheegan states hers. "I'm changing mine. I wish to move on from my past."

Kyle's face drips with displeasure. "If you feel strongly about this, Rheegan, then I will allow it. The truth is it can be unsettling to shift your attention during a sojourn. You've already taken part in two sweats holding a different intention. The spirits are trying to bring you a message. Changing now could be disruptive."

Rheegan crosses her bony arms over her chest and confirms her new intention.

Kyle begrudgingly accepts.

Next comes Erick.

"Erick, let me welcome your spirit to the circle. What is your intention?" Shaman Kyle lightly plays his flute as he awaits a response.

Only I can sense the increase in Erick's heart rate. Externally, he seems totally chill.

"I want to unplug from the rat race. I need to cleanse my aura of any toxicity."

It takes every ounce of self-control I don't possess to keep from busting into a fit of giggles. He's practically parroting Dean. However, he added some new material. This Harper guy is a quick learner. I wonder how he would react to actually living in a place like Sedona? A mini mind movie unfolds . . .

"Mitzy, it is Mitzy, isn't it?"

And I've drifted off once again. "Yes. I was really tuned in to the messages I was receiving. It feels like I need to get in touch with my inner child. Does that make sense?"

Shaman Kyle carefully places his flute in his lap and nods as only a guru can. "It does. That is deep work, Mitzy. I hope you are committed to processing what may come up for you."

"Oh, totally."

Shaman Kyle's face registers instant disappointment, and his wispy brown mustache sags. For a split second it's easy to picture the disgruntled, unruly grey mustache of Silas in its place.

Kyle and Two Trees wrap up the drumming circle and we're instructed to get a good night's sleep to prepare for tomorrow's journey.

The bright moonlight guides us to our yurt and, once inside our sketchy accommodations, I rifle through my suitcase, find the hidden pocket, and extract my backup.

Erick whistles softly. "Juvenile delinquent barely begins to describe you, Moon. When did you get that phone?"

"I have a few burners in the giant closet in my old apartment. Grams is the one who told me to pack it."

He rubs a hand across his face and shakes his head. "I'll say it again. I am extremely grateful that you and your grandmother use your powers for good. You'd be a diabolical duo on the other side of the equation."

"I'll take that as a compliment, Harper."

"You think you'll get any reception?"

"Only one way to find out. I already got a message in my ring from Pyewacket, so I better at least try."

He picks up the drum he brought from the circle and slowly taps out a rhythm.

"What are you doing?"

Erick tilts his head as though it should be obvious. "Making a little background noise. It's not like these units are exactly soundproof."

"Excellent point."

Placing the call, I'm not surprised when Pyewacket immediately answers. However, the connection is terrible, and I can only hope my apology gets through. He's waving something in front of the camera, but the image keeps freezing and disappearing because of our poor connection.

Hopefully, that wasn't a clue.

I offer a regretful goodbye and promise to call from an area with better reception tomorrow.

It might be my imagination, or there may have been an actual hiss before the call dropped completely.

As I struggle to climb into my side of the floor-mattress bed contraption, Erick crosses his arms in that yummy way that makes his biceps bulge and stares down at me. "Oh, how the mighty have fallen."

"What?"

"It looks to me like you're going straight to bed. Am I seeing that correctly?" Mischief sparkles in his deep-blue eyes.

"What are you up to, Harper? Weren't you the one commenting about how *thin* these walls are?"

He laughs and takes a deep breath. "What I meant was, it's very unlike you to simply climb into bed and give up. Everyone else is going to be tucked into their yurts. It seems like the perfect time to poke around. Did I mention how many phones were in the safe inside the headquarters camper when Desert Flower opened it to add ours?"

There's fresh intel, and I want it. "You have my attention." He helps me to my feet and fills in the blank. "There were six phones already inside. One for each of the sojourners present at this evening's drum circle, plus one extra. Seems to me if Luminous Being had left the retreat early, she would've taken her phone with her."

As he's talking, I tug on my socks and shoes. "Looks like Harper and Moon are getting into this."

He grins. "You better believe it."

"Hold on. I'm going to grab the dreamcatcher Silas gave me. I can speak her name and, if she's here, we'll have assistance for the next hour."

To his credit, Erick does not mock the alchemy. "Sounds good."

When I reach into my carry-on to retrieve the special dreamcatcher, I get a nasty surprise. "It's broken! Look." An instant replay of my call with Pyewacket flickers through my mind. "That's what Pye was trying to show me! He must've known it was broken."

"That cat is something else." Erick takes the two pieces, still tangled together by the woven threads, and sighs. "Definitely can't be fixed. Will it still work — like this?"

"Worth a try." I hold the web with both hands and softly speak my request. "Help us locate Luminous Being."

Nothing.

My husband smiles encouragingly. "Anything?"

"Nope. Zilch." I tuck the broken talisman into my backpack and take a deep breath. "Looks like we'll have to do this the old-fashioned way, Harper. You with me?"

"Always." Erick takes my hand and leads me into the cool night.

Starting at the dying embers of our drum-circle fire, we attempt to make a methodical search. First, we carefully circle the trailer-based headquarters, and then proceed down the path through the yurts.

Rheegan's is the first. Soft chanting floats through the night air, and a single flickering candle flame casts her shadow against the canvas.

The next yurt must contain Jonathan and Desiree. They're engaged in a whispered argument. She's angry about him ignoring us at the creek and he's referencing the promise she made about keeping to themselves during the retreat and avoiding entanglements.

Glancing at Erick in the moonlight, I shrug my disinterest and we continue. The next yurt is dark and silent. Could be Winter and Ivan went directly to bed, but when we see illumination spilling from the next cloth dwelling, Erick grips my shoulder and leans down. "Should we search this one?"

I nod.

He motions for me to enter and then makes several hand signals, including one where he points two fingers at his eyes and then gestures to the horizon. I don't have time to explain my lack of hand-signal knowledge, so, going with my gut, I assume that means he'll keep watch while I search.

Have you ever attempted to quietly unzip a zipper? Yeah. Not so much.

Thankfully, the couples on either side of the empty yurt are too preoccupied, and no one pops out to investigate.

I slip inside the darkened structure. Fortunately, the flap covering the peak of the yurt is either purposely or accidentally flicked open. Lovely moonlight spills into the enclosure and aids my search.

The space looks abandoned at first glance, so I lean into my extra senses in hopes of discovering more.

There are no bags on the bamboo-matt floor, no shoes by the door, and no towel on the hook. I'm afraid if this is where Luminous Being was housed, it's been thoroughly cleaned out.

Maybe she did pack up her stuff and leave early.

An unseen force pulls me toward the mattress, and I lie on the floor and shove my arm beneath. As I clumsily slide around, my hand bumps into a piece of cloth, and I grasp it. There's something wrapped in the cloth, but I worry I've already been inside too long.

I shove the bundle into my pocket and rejoin Erick outside the yurt. Hoping to cover our tracks, I close the flap with as much stealth as possible.

Erick tugs me toward Winter and Ivan's place, and their raised voices carry a harsh edge.

Ivan is admonishing Winter, once again, for abandoning his vow of silence, and Winter is asking him what he thinks really happened to Luminous.

Reaching out, I grip Erick's arm. "This could get interesting." My whisper seems to echo in the silent night. And then I hear a footstep.

Running with the first wild idea that hits me, I step away from the sojourner's yurt and collapse onto the ground.

Since Erick can't read my mind, he has no idea what's going on and crouches next to me in genuine concern. "Mitzy?"

The next voice I hear is not a surprise to me. "Erick? Why are you and Mitzy out of your yurt?" Shaman Kyle's tone is not calm and peaceful; in fact, it's packed with genuine irritation.

As Erick turns to answer, I pinch his hand. Hopefully, he'll figure out that means this is all a ruse.

"We took a walk in the stillness of the moonlight. At the creek, we turned around and we were on our way back to our hut — she just collapsed."

Shaman Kyle steps closer and gazes down. "The energy of the drum circle may have been too much for her." He crouches beside me. "Mitzy, it's Shaman Kyle. Are you experiencing a vision?"

I wasn't. But this sounds like a great cover story. "There are so many images."

Shaman Kyle inhales, floats his hands in the air above me, and hums softly. "Deep breaths. Take a deep breath and let the images come. The more you resist, the more of your energy they will consume."

Without warning, my pretend vision turns into a full-blown clairvoyant episode. "There's a boy.

He's about ten. He's wearing a yellow robe and bowing to a man in all white."

The vision transforms as Kyle grumbles.

"It's changing. I think it's the same boy, but he's older, maybe seventeen or eighteen. He's running. Running from someone — wait — after someone." A spasm of sorrow grips my body. "There are taillights disappearing into the night."

Kyle rockets to his feet. "Who told you this? I'm not amused."

My husband gently shakes my shoulders. "Mitzy. Mitzy, can you hear me?"

Sitting up, I suck in fresh air and struggle to slow my heart rate. "Did I say it out loud? Did I tell you?"

Erick opens his mouth, but before he can comment, Shaman Kyle reprimands me. "I don't appreciate mockery. In the future, if Desert Flower feels the need to share privileged information about my traumatic childhood, I would appreciate it if you would have the decency not to turn it against me."

What's his deal? "I have no idea what you're talking about, Kyle. Desert Flower didn't tell me anything. Like, we were just on a walk . . . and then . . ."

I can sense the shift in his energy. He's worried about my vision's authenticity. The guy in the images was definitely a younger version of Kyle.

"There's no need to discuss this any further. I'll escort you two back to your yurt. Sleep is important to the process."

Erick helps me to my feet. And Kyle marches us to our dwelling.

I'll bet Desert Flower is gonna get an earful when Kyle gets back to the camper.

Time to get some zzzs, and prepare for the sojourn ahead.

As I lie within the flimsy yurt, the familiar nighttime sounds of the desert hold no comfort. The cicadas seem to chant an ominous warning, and the wind whispers dangerously in the cottonwoods. A lone coyote howls in the distance — a sound I used to love — but tonight my blood runs cold.

Restless sleep finally pulls me under, but rather than offering an escape from the mounting dread, this too fills me with fear.

Something slinks in the shadows of the dreamworld, and, as it moves closer, my heart races. Suddenly, I'm face to face with an angry caracal. His fierce eyes seem to hold me in a spell. The black tufts on his sharply pointed ears twitch as he arches his back in an unfriendly pose.

"Pye? Are you upset? I tried to call you." My dream-pleading has no effect.

The scars across his left eye and cheek appear

almost fresh, and, without warning, he speaks. "Betrayal."

The voice is haunting and deep. The single word turns to ice in my veins, and my muscles seem to contract in on themselves.

"Who was betrayed? You? Did I betray you?"

Large hands softly shake my shoulders. "Mitzy, wake up. I think you're having a nightmare."

"Where's Pyewacket? He was here. He— He was so upset with me."

Erick pushes the hair back from my sweaty fore-head and kisses my cheek. "You were dreaming. You must've been dreaming about Pyewacket. Was there a message?"

Sitting up, I throw the covers off my body and hug my knees to my chest. "It was so real. I could feel his presence. He spoke."

Erick strokes circles on my back. "He always talks to you. You told me you're able to understand him better every day."

Leaning into his comforting arm, a shaky breath lifts my chest. "No. This time, he *actually* talked. He said 'betrayal.' And there was hurt in his eyes. Like I betrayed him."

Erick pulls me into an embrace and kisses the top of my head. "Hey, there's a lot going on. All I know is that Pyewacket misses you and loves to help you solve cases. I'm sure the dream is his version of a long-distance clue. Just tack it up on your mental murder wall and we'll leave it at that. You've got to get some sleep."

Nodding my head, I flop onto the pillow, as Erick curves around me like a big spoon.

CHAPTER 12

ACCORDING TO MY HUSBAND it's unbelievably 0400 hours, which is 4:00 a.m. for the rest of us, and Shaman Kyle is striding among the yurts playing his flippin' flute!

I like morning about as much as a certain orange-striped tabby cat likes Mondays. "I'm not getting out of this floor bed. He can't make me!"

"Remember, Moon, we're here to win friends and influence people."

Despite my aggravation at the early morning, new-age version of a reveille, I grin as I roll out of bed. The fantastic news is that when I sleep on a mattress, which is literally on the floor, I don't have far to fall.

We dress quickly and head for the outhouse and open-air sink facility.

Once again, I'm reminded of the urgency in solving this case. The sooner we figure out what happened to Luminous Being, the sooner we can get the heck out of here and return to indoor plumbing — and room service!

Eight large wooden tables with bench seats populate the breakfast area. Desert Flower encourages each sojourner, or pair of sojourners, to sit at a separate table. Let's hope she'll excuse me for ignoring that request.

Once I grab my breakfast of plain, sticky oatmeal and mixed-berry topping, I take a seat beside Rheegan.

Erick catches my eye and goes to work distracting Desert Flower.

Better use my time wisely. "Hey, last night, one of the other sojourners mentioned someone named Luminous Being. We haven't met her yet. Is she another solo seeker?"

Thank heaven for psychic senses!

Rheegan totally recognizes the name and is desperately searching the recesses of her mind for an answer that will not implicate her, but will make me go away. "Maybe she was here the week before us. I keep to myself. And if she was here on an exclusive package, she would do her sweats separate from everyone else."

An interesting amount of information about

someone she claims she doesn't know. "Exclusive? I didn't know that was an option. Why would someone choose to do a sweat by themselves?"

"Oh, it's only if Shaman Kyle recommends it. Certain energies can't intermingle. Maybe if she was dealing with something really heavy, he didn't want that energy in the sweat lodge with other sojourners."

At a whopping $8,000 per person for a retreat package, plus $2,000 for the exclusivity upgrade, I'm surprised Shaman Kyle doesn't *recommend* it more often. I'll keep my shock and awe to myself. "Oh, cool. Why did Desert Flower call you a nomad?"

Before she can answer, a now-familiar voice resounds behind me. "Mitzy, please join Erick at your private table. I encourage everyone to embrace a time of quiet contemplation during breakfast. After all, you are here on a spiritual journey, not to have a social mixer."

Oooh! Sick spiritual burn, Shaman. I resist the temptation to roll my eyes and instead take my meager rations to the table with my husband.

Erick grins happily as I climb onto the bench across from him. "Did you sleuth out any goodies, missus?"

Oh brother. "I did. But we've been instructed to

observe quiet contemplation during breakfast, so I guess I'll have to tell you later, *mister*."

Taking a large bite of sloppy grey oatmeal, he winks and pushes a mug of coffee toward me.

"Thank the powers that be. I was worried they were going to make us drink some kind of boiled twig tea."

Erick arches an eyebrow and stops chewing.

Taking the mug in two hands, I inhale and pretend to cry. "No. Not my precious coffee."

After breakfast, Two Trees leads us on a nature walk. We're supposed to look for messages among the rocks and plants, but our guide seems more interested in smoking his personal stash of "herb." I try to hang back and talk to Desiree and Jonathan, but they are definitely sticking to their agreement to avoid entanglements. They're having none of my small talk.

Winter has once again taken up his public vow of silence, and Ivan seems more depressed than usual.

Slowing my pace and dragging Erick to the very back of the queue, I share my intel. "Rheegan definitely knows more than she's saying. If I can get her alone, I think I can crack her."

He slips an arm around my waist and kisses the top of my head. "Maybe you can sit by her in the sweat lodge."

"If Shaman Kyle isn't allowing chatter at breakfast, I can't really see him going for all-out conversation in the sweat."

"Fair point. Let's focus on getting through this Southwest sauna, and I'll see about making inroads with Winter and Ivan at the creek this afternoon."

Pursing my lips, I grin and nod. "Is that so? I suppose that means you're leaving the impenetrable Desiree and Jonathan to me?"

He shrugs. "I figure with your special powers, you'll get information from them one way or another."

"Can confirm." Boy, do I miss Pyewacket!

When we return to camp, Shaman Kyle announces the rocks are ready and that we must all pass through the cleansing smoke of sage and sweetgrass before entering.

Rheegan strips down to her chonies, and Desiree follows suit.

I take one look at Erick and give a firm, negatory shake of my head.

Shaman Kyle gestures to me. "You may find synthetic fabrics unwelcome in the sweat lodge, Mitzy."

"No problem. Cotton T-shirt. Cotton shorts. I'm good."

Erick yanks off his T-shirt while Rheegan and Winter both stare unabashedly.

Looks like he was right about being the proper envoy with Winter and Ivan.

We each, in turn, stand before the shaman. He holds a smoking bundle of sage and sweetgrass and uses what appears to be an eagle feather (Side note: totally illegal for non-Native Americans to possess) to waft the smoke over us.

Once we've all been cleansed, to his satisfaction, he allows us into the sweat lodge one by one, taking our seats in a circle around a central pit.

The firekeeper, Two Trees, brings in one blistering rock at a time, using two deer antlers to transport the searingly hot stones from the fire outside to the pit in the center of the sweat lodge. Seven rocks are placed, and then Shaman Kyle pours water over the rocks.

A loud hiss and sizzle fills the small space as steam rises. He closes the entrance flap, leaving us in complete darkness, and gives the final instructions from *outside* the sweat lodge. "Settle into the womb of Mother Earth. Open yourselves to the spirit. Do not resist any messages that are delivered."

Even though I'm certain we're meant to observe silence, I lean toward Winter and whisper, "How long do we have to stay in here?"

Since he's in a public space, he seems to be

playing the vow of silence card. He presses one finger against my leg.

"One? One hour?"

He grumbles affirmatively. I feel like fainting again.

The air is so thick, I can almost chew it. The steam and heat are palpable. How I long for the dry heat of the desert. I can't imagine surviving an hour in this space. Although, on the upside, my vision is adjusting.

Leaning to my right, I whisper to Erick. "Did you bring any water in?"

He shakes his head, tilts to his right, and asks the same question of Rheegan.

You'd think he'd stung her with a scorpion.

She jumps, gasps, and stares at him in horror. "No talking."

Super. Trapped in what amounts to a steam oven for an hour with no water and a decree of silence.

This is feeling like a recurring nightmare I had as a child. Suffocation seems like a genuine possibility.

The crew settles into a silent rhythm. Although no one is above gasping in fresh air when Two Trees opens the flap to add more scorching hot rocks!

There are three such rock-adding moments. A

second of fresh, cool air whooshes in, followed by Shaman Kyle dousing the rocks with more water and slapping the flap back down.

Each round intensifies the boiling hot experience, and my only hope of survival is tiny, shallow breaths.

When the flap opens for the final time, I can't even move. I don't believe we're actually free. It's like a behavior-modification experiment gone wrong.

Thankfully, there's a guy in here who gets me. Literally.

CHAPTER 13

AFTER WHAT SEEMS LIKE AN ETERNITY, Erick has successfully pulled me out of that nightmare of a sweat lodge, and it feels as though I've lived through a scene from Kurt Russell's *Escape from New York.*

Everyone goes straight for water. Weakness inhabits my cells. I fear I'll pass out before I'm able to pour the life-giving liquid down my throat. As my shoulders droop and the peripheral of my vision darkens, a firm hand scoops around me and lifts a cup to my lips.

In my world, these are the moments when Erick Harper exceeds all expectations and attains superhero status. He's definitely the guy I want by my side in any form of crisis.

Once hydration seeps into my body, there's an

eagerness to get to the creek. My brain is experiencing a rare occurrence. I'm more concerned with immersing my body in the cold, snowmelt water than filling my belly with what passes for food in this place.

Erick grabs his T-shirt from a bench, takes my hand, and leads the way to Beaver Creek.

A flash of memory hits me as we pass the yurt. I tug Erick to the side; slip into our tent-like quarters, and down the restorative tincture from Silas. Have I mentioned that my mentor is a genius?

The effect is nearly instantaneous. My heart rate returns to normal. My breathing is slow and even, and the oppressive, drained feeling vanishes.

Although, when I see the sparkling water ahead, I don't have the wherewithal to remove my socks and shoes. Pulling my hand from Erick's grasp, I lunge forward.

Muscular arms loop around me. "Hey, it'll take forever for your tennis shoes to dry. Let me help you out of them and make sure you don't have to wear a pair of the heels your grandmother packed."

"Yes, Officer." Collapsing onto the dusty path, I allow him to treat me like a toddler, and kiss his cheek once my bare feet are revealed.

Without a care for the rocky shore, I race into the chilly creek. My head bursts above the water like a mermaid surfacing for the first time. As I gasp for air, my whole body tingles with energy. Maybe I can attribute it to a side effect of the sweat lodge, or possibly it's simply the relief of breathing not-steamy air — but I'm pretty sure it's from the tincture of alchemical wonder.

Erick rises from the water and flicks his hair back, like every gorgeous surfer in every California beach-based movie I've ever seen — and I get a rush of entirely different tingles.

He winks at me and heads toward a large flat rock where Winter and Ivan are relaxing.

I dip my head in the water, slick my bone-white hair backward and relish the cold rivulets racing down my back. Time to get to work.

Approaching Desiree and Jonathan, I try an entirely new tactic. "Hey, I'm super new to all of this. Is it normal for there to be no drinking water inside the sweat lodge?"

"No. But don't start anything, okay?" Her head is shaved on one side, and the opposite displays bright-red bangs, dripping water onto her shoulder.

Bingo! Yahtzee! Desiree bites.

"What? Did someone complain?" I'm almost holding my breath in secret hope as I slide from casual conversation to my true target.

She looks at Jonathan and takes a deep breath. "The girl that left early, Luminous Being, she had a huge argument with Kyle about it. He kept telling her it wasn't the native way, and she threatened to report him."

For the life of me, I can't imagine who she would've reported him to, but I'm not about to slow the flow of information from the difficult-to-crack Desiree.

"Did she? I mean, did she actually report him?"

Desiree scrapes her long bangs back and shrugs.

Jonathan picks up the conversation baton. "We did our first sweat with her, and I totally picked up on some dark energy." He rubs both hands along his tight fade, and yawns. "There was something off about her. I mentioned it to Shaman Kyle, and that might've had something to do with her having to enact her exclusivity package option. She was pretty rude to me in the drum circle that night." His spiky black hair glints in the bright afternoon sun.

"Rude? How?"

Jonathan bites his lower lip, and Desiree takes over. "She was kind of entitled, you know? Like, she always had to be first in line for breakfast. She always had to sit next to Two Trees at the drum circle. And, she was always having private conversations with Shaman Kyle. We all paid to be here, you know?" She splashes water on her face and sighs. "It wasn't right."

"It doesn't sound like it. Once Kyle put her into

that exclusivity package, did she do another sweat by herself, or did she leave right away? Seems like someone who loves to be the center of attention wouldn't like having the spotlight taken away, you know?" I add Desiree's little phrase in an attempt to create more bonding.

Jonathan nods enthusiastically. "No doubt. No doubt. She only had one sweat by herself, then she took off."

"Wow. She sounds like a real piece of work. I can't believe you guys were so magnanimous. Impressive."

A self-satisfied smile spreads across Desiree's face, and Jonathan's grin quickly joins it. He adds, "Yeah, I live for that. People trying to work the system at a spiritual retreat."

Having collected more information in the last few minutes than in the entirety of our previous time at the retreat, I'm feeling rather proud of myself. Glancing around the creek to locate my husband, my brief bravado vanishes.

Erick is standing in the creek up to his waist, splashing water over his bare chest and laughing like a model in a Banana Republic ad.

Winter is circling him like a hungry shark on the hunt, and Ivan is smiling from ear to ear and talking a mile a minute. Time to reel in my accidental Adonis.

"I so appreciate you guys sharing that with me. I definitely don't want to be difficult or ruin anyone else's experience, you know?"

Jonathan nods. "No doubt. No doubt."

Desiree smiles, grips his hands, and leads him to the other shore.

Wading through the water, I try to catch Erick's eye, but he seems totally preoccupied with whatever story he's currently pantomiming for his rapt audience.

If at first you don't succeed, try, try again, an oldie but a goodie.

Pretending to trip over a submerged rock, I let out a soft scream and tumble forward.

Works like a charm.

Seconds later, strong arms pull me to the surface, and as I'm about to plant a kiss on my savior's lips, the voice of Shaman Kyle breaks the spell. "Are you injured, Mitzy?"

Reeling back in horror, I sputter and struggle to free myself from the grip of this imposter.

Seconds later, the real Erick slips a muscular arm around my waist and waves off the shaman. "Thanks, Kyle. I've got her."

Winter snickers and Rheegan gasps.

"Thanks, Shaman Kyle." Hopefully, my overemphasis of his fake title will smooth over the mini-scandal. Yeesh!

As we return from the creek, Erick whispers, "Fake some kinda injury when we get to the picnic tables. Then you can head straight back to the yurt and try to call home. I'll grab our dinner and bring it to the tent."

"I don't think *Shaman* Kyle will approve."

Erick squeezes me. "Don't worry. I'll make some excuse about your delicate feminine constitution."

Leaning away, I wind up to punch him playfully, but he grips my hand and pulls me close. "Hey, don't be acting all violent. You'll ruin my great cover story."

"You'll pay for this, Harper."

He chuckles. "Put it on my tab, Moon."

When we reach the open eating area, I grab my stomach in pretend pain and stumble toward our dwelling.

Quick as a flash, Erick is back with two large salads and two apples. "I know it'll never rival Myrtle's Diner, but you've got to eat something."

Oh, how I miss the golden fries at my favorite local haunt back in Pin Cherry Harbor! I wave a shushing hand at him and return my attention to the screen. "Sorry I lost the call last night, Pyewacket. The reception here is terrible. We just had our first opportunity to question witnesses, so I don't have much to go on. Something about an argument—"

"RE-OW!" Game on!

"I know you're ready to solve this thing, buddy. Was it my imagination, or did you appear in my dreams?"

"Reow." Can confirm.

"Do I need to make cards, dear?" Grams holds a pen in one hand and stares pensively off-camera.

Erick places my salad on the ground beside me, and I curl up my lip and look away. He sits cross-legged, gobbling his up as though it's the very food of the gods. Waving his fork at me, he says, "Tell him what he said."

"Oh, yeah. Hold on, Grams. Pye, in the dream, you mentioned betrayal. Is that a clue to the case—" The image freezes and, before the picture can snap out of existence, I know the window has closed. Tucking the backup phone inside my pillowcase, I cross my arms and pout. "This is the worst case ever! I can barely talk to Grams and Pye, and I have to eat nothing but vegetables!"

Erick sets his half-empty bowl on the floor and guzzles water from his canteen. "It's not that bad, Moon. We're out in nature, the weather is gorgeous, and that creek — I could swim in there all day."

At the mention of the creek, my crossed arms relax, and I lean forward. "Yeah, let's actually talk about you and that creek. What was that show you were putting on for Winter and Ivan?"

He laughs uncomfortably and his cheeks flush. "It was nothing. Just playing to my audience. I needed information. They needed to feel like I was somebody they wanted to give information to."

Grabbing a leaf of lettuce from the salad with my fingers, I crunch loudly in my best Bugs Bunny imitation. "Go on, Doc."

"Initially, I got them talking about themselves. They've been together for six years, soul-bonded for two of those years, and they live in a beachside town called Cambria, California. Winter is a programmer for a startup app company, and Ivan is the chef at an exclusive bistro. He owns it too."

"Wow. I thought I was having trouble with the menu here. Imagine being a chef and having to eat that gruel they call oatmeal?"

He chuckles. "Once I got them talking, I brought up the subject of the missing girl, and they were pretty sure she left early. They mentioned an argument she had with Shaman Kyle—"

"Was it about not having water in the sweat lodge? Because that's what Desiree and Jonathan said."

My ever-patient husband nods. "Yes. I was getting to that part, but I guess I'll skip ahead. Winter said that he saw Luminous Being on the phone talking about what Kyle is getting away with. He heard someone coming and couldn't stick around to hear more."

"Wait! But you counted the phones in the safe, and we assumed that the extra phone was hers. How could she be talking on her phone if Desert Flower locked it up?"

"Maybe she brought a backup phone, like you."

Popping a tomato in my mouth, I pierce the skin with my teeth and I'm surprised by the sweet, enjoyable flavor. "Yeah, but I'm an undercover private investigator, and something of a reprobate. What was Luminous Being doing with a secret backup phone?"

Erick shrugs his shoulders. "Maybe there's a little more to her name change than Dean thought. I wish we could get our hands on that phone in the safe."

"I'm sure I could come up with a plausible emergency that would require our phones, but then we'd have to leave, and I don't think we're done investigating."

He stretches out on the floor and tucks his hands behind his head. "Same problem with my idea. I'm sure I could shoot through the lock on the safe and gain access, but that would definitely be a one-way ticket out of shaman town."

"Good one, Harper." My eyes drink in all that is

Erick Harper and, when I land on his messy hair, a smile slides across my face like butter on hot pancakes. "I like your hair like that."

He tosses it with his hand. "I brought my pomade, but I didn't see much point with all this sweat lodging and creek swimming. You don't like it slicked back?"

Setting my salad down, I crawl toward him and lace my fingers through his. "I didn't say that. Your all-business pomade style is one of the things I love about you. I was only commenting on the fact that I like this, too. I like all the Ericks. Not just business Erick."

He pulls me close, but before we can start anything truly transcendental, a commanding voice calls through the canvas. "Two Trees is about to start tonight's drum circle. I expect you both to attend."

Erick flashes his eyebrows and grins. I silently snarl at him in honor of my absent wildcat.

He answers for both of us. "Yes, Shaman."

We are the last to arrive at the drum circle, and the only spot left is between Desiree and Rheegan.

Since I didn't much care for the way Rheegan was ogling my husband at the creek, I sit next to her, and leave Erick to wedge himself in next to the icy Desiree.

Two Trees finds his rhythm, and Shaman Kyle joins with his flute.

However, only about half of the circle has added their rhythm to the mix when Shaman Kyle stops playing and announces he must depart.

"I leave you in the capable and rhythmic hands of Two Trees. I have to prepare myself for tomorrow's sweat. May you all receive a blessed and recuperative rest this evening. Aho."

Desiree grumbles something quietly in Jonathan's ear, and Two Trees restarts the beat.

Shaman Kyle has only been gone for about fifteen minutes when Two Trees announces we can take our drumming to the next level with the addition of psychedelic mushrooms or edibles. He produces two plastic baggies from the pockets of his tie-dye wrap pants.

"Who wants to join me and the spirit in the sky for some next-level drumming?" Based on the overly laid-back tone of his voice, I'd say he's already a couple edibles ahead of the rest of us.

Desiree and Jonathan immediately make their excuses and leave the drum circle.

Erick grabs my hand, makes an executive decision for us, and we exit as well.

Oh well, I'm fairly certain there's no gummy or mushroom that can match the rush of true extrasensory perceptions.

My partner falls asleep instantly, but my brain is spinning. My mood ring picks now to join the party, and when I gaze into the swirling mists within the cabochon an image of my cell phone shimmers.

I thrust my hand into the pillowcase and pull out the phone. Oh, no! Seven missed calls from Headquarters.

Pulling the covers over my head and attempting to keep my voice low, I place a call to Grams and Pyewacket.

Pyewacket answers immediately.

"R-oooow-oo." Where are you?

Although the intonation is brand new, I clearly receive his message.

"Sorry, Pye. I have to keep the lights off and my voice down. I can't risk waking up Erick or getting discovered by Shaman Kyle."

One large golden eye winks and my co-conspirator moves aside so Grams can deliver her message.

"How's the investigation going? I don't like you being so far away from your wardrobe consultant. What are you wearing?"

"In bed?" Oh brother. I must keep my cool and remember to whisper. "Listen, Grams, I'm doing the best I can. We're in and out of sweat lodges. Cooling off in questionable creek water . . . I haven't really had time for a ball gown."

She ghost snorts and clutches one of her many strands of pearls. "Oh sweetie, I miss your sense of humor. Pyewacket is too sedate for my taste."

"Reeeee-ow." A warning.

"Easy, Grams. He's your only friend until I get back. Don't bite the hand that feeds you, or, in this case, I guess it would be insulting the mouth that bites you? I don't know. Anyway, I miss you guys too. We don't have much to go on. Most of the other people at the retreat seem to believe the story about Luminous leaving early. But I just don't buy it. I smell a rat."

"Reow." Can confirm. Pyewacket's broad, tan head reenters the screen, and I swear he's salivating. Perhaps mentioning vermin isn't the best reference when speaking to a half-wild caracal.

"Anyway, we did get some information about a sketchy argument, and someone overheard her possibly reporting Kyle's questionable methods. It's not much to go on. I played sick to set up my excuse for tomorrow. In the morning, I'll continue the ruse. While everyone's in the sweat lodge, I'll head out and search the surrounding area. Hopefully that will turn up something."

Distant rustling outside the yurt concerns me. My psychic senses are sleepier than usual and fail to provide additional information.

"Hey, I gotta go. Love you guys."

Pyewacket mews in a way that seems heartbro-ken, and Grams sniffles as a ghostly tear trickles from the corner of her eye.

Ending the call, I stash my secret back-up phone inside my pillowcase and feign sleep.

Erick rolls toward me and sleep-whispers to the back of my neck. "Everything okay at home?"

"So you weren't asleep."

"I may be a sound sleeper, but when someone's making clandestine calls into the pillow next to mine, it does tend to interfere with my zzzs."

Twisting toward him, I plant a kiss on his soft lips. "No more disturbances. I promise."

He returns my affection and chuckles. "At least not tonight."

"Rude."

CHAPTER 14

ERICK

THE EARLY MORNING ROUSTING from the rack
and bland food remind me too much of my time in
the Army.

To be fair, there was more discipline, and no
mention of chakras or intentions, but the general
concept of everyone doing as they were told and
functioning as a group is the same.

Mitzy opts to skip breakfast and double-down
on her fake illness from last night. The ever-
watchful eye of Kyle has prevented her from any
serious sleuthing.

Today, she plans to venture outside the camp
and see if her special abilities can give her any help
in locating Luminous.

I hate that she's headed out on her own, even if
she claims the desert was her first home. I emptied

out my backpack, filled it with some stolen rye crackers and an apple from breakfast, and it didn't take much to encourage her to lug my canteen along as well. She has her secret back-up phone, and promised to call the Tribal Police if she gets into trouble.

Fine by me. My mission is to make a great excuse for her and continue to keep everyone preoccupied with all this sweat lodge nonsense until she gets back.

"Good morning, Shaman Kyle. I'm sorry to report that Mitzy won't be joining us. Her stomach is still acting up, and she's really feeling warm. I don't think several hours in a sweat lodge will improve her situation."

"Sorry to hear that. I know the local medicine man. Would you like me to get in touch?"

I wasn't expecting this twist. "No thanks. Let's give her the day. If she's not squared away by tonight, I might take you up on that."

Holding my arms out to my side, parallel with the ground, I hold my breath while Shaman Kyle gives me the sage-smoke treatment.

The others are already inside, so I quietly take my place. A quick check of occupants reveals Mitzy isn't the only one missing.

"Ivan, where's Winter?"

Ivan blows air through his lips and shakes his

head. "He was a little too eager to break the rules last night. He and Two Trees had an after-drum-circle psychedelic experience." The light filtering through the open flap allows me to catch Ivan's smirk.

Last night, about the time Two Trees mentioned edibles, was when Mitzy and I headed back to the yurt.

"Understood. Maybe that's what has Mitzy under the weather. It would be just like her to sneak out after I nodded off." Ivan and I share a chuckle before Two Trees, looking none the worse for wear, begins loading the hot stones into the pit.

I count ten today, as opposed to the previous seven. Kyle pours the water on, closes the flap, and issues his version of wise advice.

Heat doesn't bother me. I'm not going to pretend I'd choose this as a vacation, but two tours in Afghanistan taught me how to endure pretty much anything.

Before my eyes are fully adjusted, my ears reveal a secret. Based on distance from my position, I'd have to guess Desiree and Jonathan snuck some drinking water into the lodge. Good for them.

The flap opens, rocks are added, more water is poured, and Kyle closes the flap.

I sure hope Mitzy is having luck. Today is rumored to be a longer sweat than the previous. By my estimation, we have two hours left in the lodge. That should give her enough time to search the surrounding area and return to the yurt before her absence is discovered.

When the flap next opens, I'm in for a surprise.

"Spirit has instructed me to bring you all out of the lodge. The missing energy of Winter and Mitzy has created a negative flow. We're going to take some vortex-charged red earth, and each of you will have a cleansing vortex bath. Then we'll head down to the creek. I hope everyone will attend tomorrow's sweat so that we can reinforce your original intentions and clear this cloud."

The annoyance in Kyle's voice is hard to miss. I may lack Mitzy's gifts, but I can clock frustration in a leader faster than most.

We file out of the lodge one by one. Rheegan slips a sundress on over her undergarments, and Desiree ties a towel around her waist. For some reason, she wore a bathing suit today, which doesn't make much sense based on Kyle's instruction about synthetic fabrics not being worn during the sweat. Maybe it's cotton or bamboo?

Not my problem.

Kyle produces a clay pot filled with dirt. He passes it to Rheegan and instructs her to scoop out a handful and rub it all over her body.

Sure, the dirt is red — but it's still dirt. I don't

think I'll ever get a handle on this new age stuff. Too bad Mitzy isn't here. She'd get a real kick out of this.

Jonathan wordlessly follows Rheegan's example, and while Desiree balks at the idea of rubbing dirt on her body, she's a rule follower at heart.

Must've been Jonathan who snuck the water into the lodge.

Ivan takes 'next,' and when the clay pot is handed to me, there's not much dirt left. I make the best of what's in there and smear it on my sweaty arms and legs, but I have no interest in red dirt mixing with the sweat on my back and dripping into places I'd rather it didn't.

Still no sign of Mrs. Moon.

Hopefully, that bodes well. If she finds something to be concerned about, I can only hope she follows my instruction and calls the authorities.

Desert Flower and Kyle lead us down to the creek and, when we pass the last yurt before the narrow path through the trees, Winter pops out of the dwelling and grabs Ivan's hand. "I'm feeling so much better, love. I'll join you."

Kyle glances back and exhales. I can almost sense his inner rage, but he maintains his outer Shaman-shell.

The cool waters of the creek feel incredible. I wasn't kidding when I told Mitzy I'd like to have a cabin around here somewhere. Not that there aren't plenty of cabins available in Birch County, and lakes, but I like being anonymous. After living in one place my entire life, and operating as sheriff of that same community for the last six years, there's something truly freeing about being in a place where no one knows anything about me.

As far as these folks are concerned, I'm simply Erick Harper — seeker of spiritual truth.

Ivan and Winter motion for me to join them on their flat rock.

Lazily floating toward them, an uneasy ripple hits my gut. Mitzy should be back by now. Even though Kyle cut the sweat short, she should be back.

As I climb onto the rock and smooth my hair back against my scalp, Winter leans toward me.

"I probably shouldn't say anything, but I saw Mitzy."

While my acting skills aren't great, I've learned a thing or two from watching Mitzy. "Oh, was she feeling better?"

Winter picks at his fingernails and shrugs. "She caught me using a phone down by the outhouse."

My inner actor vanishes and my seasoned lawman takes the wheel. "You had a back-up?"

Winter's large green eyes widen, and he shakes his head. "What? No. No. I found the phone in the long dry grass around the outhouse. I was going to turn it in, but it had some battery left and I was so eager to talk to our dog sitter." He presses his clasped hands to his chest and nearly cries. "We almost never leave Poco. It's been days, and I was dying for just a picture."

"I understand. Where's the phone now?"

"Mitzy took it. She seemed sure it belonged to Luminous Being." He looks down and wraps his arms around his middle.

When I used to get that body language from a suspect I was questioning, it generally meant they wanted to tell me something but were afraid.

"What else did she say?"

He licks his lips and whispers. "She told me you guys are investigators. That you suspect foul play, and you're not really here for the retreat."

There's hurt in his tone, and it's easy to imagine that he feels manipulated by my behavior yesterday. "Hey, I wish I could've told you guys about it sooner. But we weren't sure what happened, and anyone could've been a suspect."

Ivan gasps and smooths a hand across his bald head. "Did you suspect us?"

Before I can answer, Winter grabs Ivan's arm and seems almost excited at the thought. "Can you imagine, Ivee? You and I criminals!" His voice goes up an octave and a couple of decibels on that last word.

I put a hand on his leg and shake my head. "Hey, I really need you guys to keep the secret. Okay?"

Winter covers his mouth with one hand and nods. "You can count on us. We've kept our share of secrets in this lifetime."

Ivan hugs Winter close and nods in agreement. "Boy, have we. Freedom feels good though, doesn't it, Winnie?"

Winter lays his head on Ivan's shoulder and smiles. "It does."

"Did Mitzy say anything to you about where she was headed, or when she'd be back?"

Winter lurches forward and grips my arm with concern. "She only said she was gonna search all around the retreat center. Maybe she's back at the yurt. Should we go check?"

Gazing up at the position of the sun in the sky, I hold my fingers between it and the horizon line . . . Adjusting for latitude and topography, I put the time at nearly four in the afternoon. My wife has been gone for over six hours.

"Yeah, I'll go to the yurt. You guys stay here and keep Shaman Kyle occupied. Okay?"

Ivan scans the horizon. "We'd be happy to help you, Erick, but I don't see Kyle anywhere."

"Shoot. I gotta run."

They both nod, and Winter drags his fingers

across his mouth as though he's zipping his lips closed. Then he turns an imaginary key and tosses it into the creek.

On the path, the rocks poke into my bare feet, but I ignore the pain. I reach the yurt and see the flap is unzipped. My heart soars. When I look inside, the yurt is empty, and suddenly there's a thousand-pound weight on my shoulders.

Mitzy Moon, where are you?

CHAPTER 15

I SURE HOPE ERICK is doing his job covering for me back at camp. The cloudless azure sky isn't offering any relief from the unrelenting desert sun. I'll never tell him, but tossing his canteen into my backpack along with my reusable water bottle was a good idea.

A less wonderful idea — this search. Thus far it has been uneventful.

Unless you count two scorpion sightings and one late-in-the-season tarantula.

Usually, the tarantulas only appear during monsoon season, when the rain cools the earth from the intense rays of the sun. Something about the weather and mating; I don't actually remember. I only recall seeing them in late July and August.

This September sighting, under the glare of the afternoon sun, is one for the books.

Can't wait to get back to camp and tell Erick about catching Winter with a phone! As I was sneaking out of camp, I picked up a hint of movement from the corner of my eye, and, upon further investigation, discovered Winter talking on a burner phone behind the outhouse.

Me being me, I confronted him and he instantly crumbled.

He claimed to have found the phone in the grass surrounding the facilities. As he spoke, I received a clairaudient hit. The words Luminous Being assaulted my senses. I took Winter at face value and assumed the phone he'd found had been hers. After demanding the phone, he relinquished it, but threatened to rat me out for skipping my sweat.

My only hope was to buy his favor with secrets, so I told him about Erick and me being private investigators. He was absolutely thrilled. It clearly played directly into his fantasies about Erick being some kind of muscle-bound vigilante.

Anyway, all of that is hours behind me, and ahead of me there is nothing but brown grasses, spiky cat's claw, and the occasional yucca plant with its sun-dried center stock standing motionless in this still air.

My search seems like a bust.

Pausing to drink some water, I get my bearings and toy with the idea of heading back to camp—

Hold up. Are those caves?

There's a ridge off to my left. Looks to be mostly limestone. Maybe some granite. I'm no geologist. I've only heard the terms bandied about in coffee shops in Sedona.

However, regardless of the type of rock, there are some interesting markings and a distinctly dark area. Could be a cave . . .

Caves must be explored! In every movie I've ever watched about search and rescue, caves are key.

Clipping the canteen to the backpack, I march ahead with renewed hope. As I near the top of the mesa, the cave seems larger and deeper than it had from the valley floor. The circle of darkness draws me in. My curiosity is piqued.

The hairs on the back of my neck stand on end as the cool air and relative silence envelop me.

In recent years, I learned the familiar warning, which Silas calls piloerection, is loosely tied to my late mother. It's not as though she's directly sending me a message, but there's something about those shivering follicles that makes me slow my pace and reach out with my extra senses.

Just inside the mouth of the cave, I slip out of

my backpack and retrieve the flashlight Erick forced me to bring. He encouraged me to be prepared for anything, and it turns out he was on the right track.

Getting the backpack comfortably in place, I click on the halogen flashlight and continue. The hairs on the back of my neck are spiking up like porcupine quills now. I sincerely hope they're not warning me about a mountain lion curled up at the back of the cave.

Moments before I stumble over it, the beam from my torch illuminates a human shape.

Gasping, I jump backward and bump my head against the rocky ceiling.

"Oh, my gosh. That has to be—"

There's no need for me to say the name. Each of my psychic senses confirms that the motionless body on the cave floor is that of the deceased Luminous Being.

My stomach churns, and despite my many run-ins with death, this morning's breakfast-on-the-trail makes an encore appearance. Wiping my lips with the back of my hand, I take a swig from the warm canteen, rinse my mouth, and spit the water on the ground behind a large rock.

Before I call the Tribal Police, I need to take a look at the body. My stomach swirls in protest, but I mentally insist.

Stepping closer, I pick up a nearby stick and

carefully lift the multitude of blonde braids from her face.

There are no marks on her throat and no blood on her clothing. At first glance, it almost appears she could've died of natural causes. Maybe something internal, like a heart attack.

My moody mood ring finally springs to life and reveals an image of something thrown into the stone pit inside the sweat lodge.

If she was killed at camp, maybe this thing with Kyle is more serious than we suspected. But how'd she get in this cave?

Time to call the authorities. Walking back toward the mouth of the cave, I pull out my back-up phone and search for a signal.

That's when the petroglyphs catch my eye. The inner wall of the cave, and a large section of rock on the exterior, is covered with unique petroglyphs. Some symbols are familiar to me from postcards meant for tourists. There are spirals, snakes, four-legged animals with horns, and lizards. There are other symbols that seem unique to this place. When I lean into my clairaudience, I hear words like jaguar, archer, and rattlesnake.

I can't get a signal, and I don't want to leave the body without some evidence that I found her.

Picking my way around the random rocks on the floor of the cave, I head back toward the body and snap a few pictures — purely for evidentiary reasons. Once again, my stomach heaves in protest, but I keep things under control. Sliding the phone into my back pocket, I notice a shadow passing over the mouth of the cave. Assuming cloud cover means impending rain, I hurry to exit and get back to camp before the dry riverbed I had to cross turns into a raging arroyo.

Imagine my surprise, when—

"That's far enough, little lady. I'm afraid I can't let you leave."

If only I hadn't been so distracted fighting my nausea, I might've had a little warning of this twist.

"Hey! I am so lost. I came up to look at the petroglyphs and got totally turned around. Can you point me toward the main trail?" The sound of my voice in my ears is thin and fake. There's absolutely no way this guy will buy what I'm selling, but you can't blame a gal for trying.

The silhouette at the cave entrance shakes its head. "Like I said, I'm afraid I can't let you leave. You go ahead and hand me that phone, and have a seat."

"Phone? I don't have a phone."

"Look, I don't know who you are, but you've seen too much. You can hand me the phone and buy yourself some time, or I can shoot you right now."

Not sure how I missed the gun in his hand this whole time, but it's the only thing I can see now.

"Yeah, sorry. It's new and—" I've got to learn when to shut my mouth! I pull the phone from my back pocket and take a step toward him.

"Hold it right there. Toss me the phone."

"But the screen might—"

"Listen, honey, dead women make no calls. Toss me the phone or I shoot."

I toss him the phone.

He snatches it out of the air like the evil villain that he is, and I wonder how much time I bought myself.

"Have a seat on the ground." He gestures to the dirt with his gun.

"Sure. You got it."

I step backward, lower myself to the ground, and press my backpack against the cave wall.

He keeps the gun trained on me while he removes his own backpack. If I wasn't so terrified, I'd be a little impressed with his dexterity. Once he's removed the pack, he gets out a roll of duct tape and my mood darkens.

He rolls the tape to me. "Tape your ankles together — tight."

Taking the tape, I attempt to follow instructions. However, my mind wanders as I imagine

Erick being impressed by how "prepared for any-thing" this guy is.

"Tighter."

"All right."

I have a bit of trouble tearing the tape when I finish, but once I do, he comes closer.

The light spilling through the cave entrance shows me the reddish-brown hair of a man in his forties. The cut is short and professional. He has no facial hair, and the eyes are dark, maybe hazel. Maybe brown. He smells of sweat and earth. I'm too shook to gather any psychic intel.

He sets his gun down out of my reach and tapes my wrists together — snuggly. As he tears off one final piece of the sticky grey tape, I know beyond a shadow of a doubt that it's going over my mouth. Honestly, it's probably for the best. With the fear pulsing through my veins, I'm only likely to say something foolish that will shorten the hours, or perhaps minutes, I have left on this planet.

If ever there were a moment when I wished my special abilities included super strength or laser vi-sion, it's now.

The gummy tape seals over my mouth and sticks brutally to my cheeks.

He retrieves his gun and stands.

"I'm going to go pick up a friend for you. If you behave yourself, I'll kill him first. If not—"

There's no need for him to finish the sentence. I've always been pretty good at Mad Libs.

Erick No Middle Name Harper, if you're looking for a time to sprout some psychic senses, right this minute would be fantastic.

CHAPTER 16
ERICK

IF KYLE DID SOMETHING to Mitzy—

My concerned jog breaks into a panicked run. As I near the small trailer, raised voices snag my attention like a cheap fishing lure.

Slowing my pace, I step into the shadows near the camper and move closer, careful to stay out of sight.

"I have spoken to the tribal elders. They will vote tonight. All of this will be gone tomorrow. You are not keeping the old ways alive. Your promises were lies. This is cultural destruction, and the Yavapai-Apache people will not stand for it."

I don't recognize the voice, but the cadence hints at Native American.

"I signed a lease. Trudee Baca gave specific permission for me to be on this land. You can't kick me off. The lease is my permission."

Shaman Kyle has finally lost his cool. The aggravation in his voice makes it seem like this may not be the first conversation he's had with the other man.

"Trudee Baca does not speak for the whole council. I will present this evidence. You are twisting our traditions for money. A new vote will be taken. We will tolerate no more of your lies, Kyle."

Kyle grumbles loudly as I reach the edge of the trailer and peer around to get a look at the other party.

"You listen to me, Smith. Trudee Baca signed the lease. She owns this land, and she gave me permission. Her signature was notarized!"

The Native American man is of small stature, but he speaks with a confidence that belies his height. "You are showing your true nature, Kyle. No one owns Mother Earth."

The Native American man makes a symbol with his hand that must tie into a sacred gesture of his people. "Pack your things. Tomorrow you will be gone."

Kyle balls up both his fists, and my concern takes over. Stepping into the sun as though I've just arrived, I introduce myself. "Hey, I'm Erick Harper.

I don't believe we've met." I reach my hand toward the Yavapai-Apache man whose salt-and-pepper buzz cut gleams in the sun.

"Greetings, Erick Harper. I'm Peter Smith, but you can call me The Bag Man." He laughs casually.

Kyle's jaw clenches as his eyes fill with anger.

Stepping closer to The Bag Man, I have to ask. "You have to tell me how you got the nickname."

Peter slaps me on the back and leads me away from the fuming fake shaman.

"I used to be a troublemaker, in my misspent youth." He chuckles, and I laugh along.

"I had a couple of good-for-nothing friends who convinced me to rob the local food market. The three of us yanked down our masks, went in, and pulled out our airsoft guns. The old woman behind the counter was having none of it. She grabbed a shotgun from below the counter, and my two friends ran as fast as a pair of scared antelope. Left me holding the bag."

Sincere laughter grips me. "I'm sorry to laugh, Mr. Smith. Those friends really were good-for-nothing."

He grins good-naturedly. "Call me The Bag Man. Everyone does. I am sorry to cut your retreat short, but this abomination must come to an end."

"To be honest, I overheard the conversation. Is it true that Kyle is misrepresenting your customs?"

Peter nods. "For sure. For sure. The woman who he claims gave her blessing was taken in by his lofty promises. She is in her final years and has become too trusting as she slips away from us to join the ancestors. If she knew how people were being treated . . . Water is always given during a sweat. A sweat is not meant to torture a soul. And no one should pay for a sweat."

Pushing people to the brink of dehydration could be dangerous. Didn't Dean mention something about Luminous Being having escaped from a cult? Maybe something about Kyle's methods scared her into reporting him to the tribe? Definitely something to tell Mitzy — when I find her. When, not if.

"I'm looking into a couple of disappearances and need the help of the Tribal Police. Do you think you could introduce me?"

"Me? Nah. Got important family business. You tell them The Bag Man sent you. I have to pick up my grandson. He's specially abled, and the bus drops him about a mile from our house. I meet him every day, so he doesn't get lost. If I leave now, I can take a shortcut across the land and just make it."

"You walked here?"

Peter lifts his small hands in the air and shrugs. "I use what the Creator gave me. I am blessed to have working legs. Trying to take things that didn't belong to me was a bad choice. Now I walk the straight and narrow on my own two feet." He gestures toward the dirt road. "Head back down the main road, turn right by the broken fence post, and you'll see four buildings. Nice to meet you, Mr. Harper."

"Nice to meet you, Bag Man."

He snickers as he walks off in the direction of the creek.

As I walk toward Kyle, I don't plan on pulling any punches. "Kyle, where's Mitzy?"

"What? You said she wasn't feeling well. Isn't she in your yurt?"

Decision time. I'm going to go with the truth. That's always been my default.

"Mitzy and I didn't come here for the retreat. We came here to find Luminous Being. Her boyfriend, Dean, hired us. Mitzy wasn't under the weather this morning. She went out searching for the missing woman."

Kyle crosses his arms tightly and looks away. "Like the other sojourners told you, Luminous left early."

"Then why is her phone in the safe?"

He spins, and the confused look in his eyes seems genuine. I could really use Mitzy right now.

"How do you know her phone's in the safe?"

"I followed Desert Flower when she added our

phones to the mix." Gesturing toward the small camper, I add, "Open the safe if you don't believe me."

He inhales sharply. "I will."

Kyle storms into the trailer, crouches next to the safe, and furiously punches the code on the keypad. When he swings the door open, I step forward, reach into the safe, and grab the pink bejeweled phone case.

"Hey, put that back."

"This is her phone. Isn't it?"

"I don't know. Maybe. I don't really pay attention to things like that." He fidgets nervously.

"And why is that? Too busy grifting your sojourners?"

He attempts to stand, but I place a firm hand on his shoulder and shove him back down. "I'm going to the Tribal Police to request their assistance in looking for Luminous Being, and now Mitzy. If it turns out you're responsible for what happened to either of them, you're going to regret it."

He does not try to stand, and his shaky breathing appears authentic.

Slipping the recovered phone in my pocket, I jog back to the yurt and change into long pants and a dry shirt. We may be searching until after dark, and I've learned how quickly the temperature drops after sunset in the desert.

Last of all, I reach behind the felt lining, retrieve my gun case, and slip the pistol into the back of my waistband.

Grabbing the keys, I head through the eating area and snag someone's refillable water bottle. It feels full, and that's all that matters to me.

The Rubicon chews up the road, so I almost miss the broken fence post. Slamming on the brakes, I wait for the dust to settle on the bumpy dirt road. I back up, make the right turn, and shortly several nondescript tan buildings loom into view.

A weathered placard over the doorway on the central building indicates Tribal Police headquarters.

Walking in, I'm surprised to find one lone officer watching a video on his phone. He drops his phone and rockets to his feet when he catches sight of me. "Who are you?"

"The Bag Man sent me." Might as well try it.

The officer laughs openly. "I'm Karl Vincent. How can I help you?"

"Officer Vincent, I need to report two missing women. One has been missing for several days. The other went missing about 11:00 a.m. I don't know the area, and The Bag Man said you'd be able to assist me in mounting a search." I take a little freedom with The Bag Man's words, but part of me feels it's in the spirit of his intention.

"You'll need to file a missing person's report. And wait at least twenty-four hours for the second lady. Then you can file one on her too."

"Officer Vincent, I'm a former sheriff. I know the law inside and out. But I also suspect foul play. The first woman who went missing, Luminous Being, was at the retreat on the tribal land Shaman Kyle is using. She may have reported him to the council. He hasn't been observing your sacred traditions with the authenticity he promised. If the council votes to kick him off the land, Kyle will be out of a sizeable chunk of cash. The second woman, who went missing this morning, is my wife. We're private investigators now, and she went looking for Luminous Being. I know it's not evidence, but something's wrong. I feel it in my gut."

To my surprise, Officer Vincent nods. "I know that feeling. I got that feeling when my wife went into labor two months ago. I was on the other side of the land, following up on some vandalism, and I just felt it. I got in my car and drove straight back to our house. I got there in time to cut the umbilical cord." He grins proudly and his eyes shine with emotion.

"Congratulations."

"Thank you . . . What's your name?"

"Oh, Erick Harper. Sorry. I should've introduced myself. I guess I'm more concerned about my wife than I thought."

"I'll follow you back to this retreat. Is that what you called it?"

"Yeah. We can walk from there, unless you have quads."

Officer Vincent laughs loudly. "Don't we wish? When push comes to shove, we pull out the old nags. A paint and a half-wild mustang. Otherwise we drive our circa 1990s cruisers on the dirt roads, like everyone else."

He follows me out the front door and climbs into his cruiser. Remarkably well maintained for her age.

Before he shuts the door, I point toward the Rubicon. "That's me there."

As we drive back toward Shaman Kyle and the camper, the knot in my stomach tightens.

Time is running out. I can feel it.

CHAPTER 17

My captor vanishes. The duct tape is hurting my wrists and making my face itch. Sitting alone in the cool semi-darkness, I'm uncomfortably aware of the corpse sharing my shade.

I have no idea what that man meant by picking up a friend for me, and I don't intend to stick around long enough to find out.

I've seen enough hostage movies to know that the madman could return any minute. I have to make the absolute best use of the time I have. Based on my distance from camp, shouting for help would be useless. Therefore, as much as this strip of tape across my mouth annoys me, it's not a priority.

Scanning the dim interior for a jagged rock edge, I find what I'm looking for and scoot across the cave floor.

On the silver screen, it always looks so easy. You rub your wrists across the sharpened edge of whatever, and your bonds fall to the ground.

Let me be the first to tell you, it's way harder than it looks!

I'm sawing away, like I'm on a *New Yankee Workshop* weekend marathon, and I'm getting nowhere.

Another movie trope shattered.

An image of my curmudgeonly mentor flashes to mind.

Mr. Willoughby taught me how to remove metal handcuffs with an alchemical working, and when I was trapped in that bank heist last year he claimed the same teaching could get me out of a zip-tie restraint. May as well see what it can do for duct tape. I've got nothing to lose.

I remember Silas Willoughby's words like it was yesterday. "The basis of all alchemical solutions is transmutation. In this situation, the position of the lock must simply be reformed."

Let's see if I can *reform* some tape.

I feel the tape around my wrists — feel the adhesive sticking to my skin. Next, I visualize ice melting from the heat in my hand, like Silas taught me. Now I begin to soften that tape and feel the adhesive give way.

The grey bands imprisoning my wrists slowly dissolve.

Excitement causes me to lose focus and stalls the process. Several deep breaths later, I'm able to quiet my mind and finish this handy bit of alchemy.

The tape practically drips to the cave floor.

Next stop, my feet. Fortunately, I did a fairly terrible job. I'm almost convinced I could wriggle my feet out of the tape if I wanted to. However, finding an edge, picking it free, and unwinding it is highly satisfying.

No sign of my captor, so I'll take the time to re-move the final piece before I head out. My last order of escape business is to attempt a careful removal of the tape covering my mouth. Despite my gentle movements, removing the adhesive strip from my face is far more painful than any small Band-Aid.

Now I have to climb to higher ground and get a phone signal. He may have taken the phone from my back pocket, but I still have the phone I confis-cated from Winter in the backpack.

Moving as stealthily as possible, I approach the mouth of the cave. There's no sign of my captor.

Exiting the cave, I search for a route to climb to the top of the rocky outcrop that encompasses this cavern.

The unflinching sun still rules the sky, and the

contrast between the cool cave interior and the brutal desert sun baking my shoulders is shocking. The cloudless blue above me stretches in all directions.

Limestone, or more likely some type of sandstone, is not great for climbing. There are loose rocks everywhere, and I have to endure several false starts and a skinned knee.

Finally, reaching the top of the hill, I crouch behind a large boulder and extract the phone that once belonged to Luminous.

It hadn't occurred to me before, but it might be a good idea to check the last number she called. Which would be the one BEFORE Winter's call to his dog sitter, for those of you playing along at home.

Thankfully, this old flip phone has zero security.

The last number called was someone named Ethan Vods.

I tap the number and wonder if I dare ask this person for help.

"Who is this? How did you get this phone?"

The voice on the other end of the line is unmistakable, but I learned a valuable piece of information.

My captor's name is Ethan Vods.

Before I can end the call, the battery dies!

I've wasted my one chance at a rescue on a hunch.

If I climb down, there's an absolutely excellent chance of crossing paths with Ethan Vods as I attempt to sneak back to camp.

If I head off in a different direction, I could be lost in the desert and die of exposure.

What a great bunch of options.

Seems like I'll have to take my chances with Ethan Vods.

Returning the phone to my backpack in case I need it for evidence, I slip the straps over my shoulders and risk the climb down.

Once again, losing my footing, I slide, and scrape the side of my left leg. Now I have a matching set of wounds on that leg.

When I reach the mouth of the cave, I hurry down the relatively safe incline to the floor of the desert.

In the middle of no-man's-land, yards from even the most meager tree cover, I hear approaching voices.

"Where are you taking me? What could you possibly have against me? I don't even know you."

Who is that?

"Keep talking, and you'll be dead before we make it back to the cave."

That threatening voice would be Ethan Vods.

"Cave? You can't mean the room of the ancestors? You are not allowed to enter that space without a medicine man."

A scuffle ensues.

"Don't shoot. Don't shoot. I'll stop talking."

I don't recognize the captive's voice as anyone from camp. I'm curious about where Ethan picked up this new guy.

If I wasn't so freaked out, I could try my hand at the invisibility working, but that ship has already sailed halfway across Last Hope Harbor. An immature cat's claw and a couple of soap-tree yuccas are the only nearby cover.

Crouching behind the brush, I literally cross my fingers.

Footsteps approach.

Harsh laughter knifes through the late afternoon heat that is sucking the moisture from my skin.

"You're determined to be more trouble than you're worth. Come out from behind that sad little bush or I'll shoot you where you sit."

Standing, I raise my hands in the air, but my snarky center gets the best of me. "Go ahead. From everything you've said, you plan on killing me anyway. At least if you shoot me out here, someone might hear the shot and find my body. Which is more than I can say for Luminous."

The Native American man being propelled by Ethan Vods lurches unsteadily toward me. It's easy to assume there's a gun at his back.

"Huh. Is that so? If you don't care about your own life, maybe you have some kind of savior complex. Believe me, I know the type. Maybe I'll just shoot this guy." Ethan chuckles wickedly as he aims the gun at my co-captive.

The man's dark eyes brim with fear, but the energy radiating from him is one of worry and concern for others. He genuinely seems unconcerned about his own life. But there is someone else—

"I tell you what, Ethan." That gets his attention. His eyes widen, and his devil-may-care attitude slips, if only for a moment. "Since I've got a firm expiration date, you may as well tell me why you killed Luminous. We can call it my last wish."

His nostrils flare, as he moves closer with his new captive. "I'll tell you in the cave."

"No dice. Story first, then I walk." I have no idea if he'll import what I'm exporting, but I'm absolutely gonna put it on offer, regardless.

"Fine. You want the truth, Blondie?" His stare is cold, unflinching.

One of the many things I've learned in the hundreds of hours of film I've consumed is that you have to build rapport with your captor. "My name is Mitzy Moon. Not Blondie. Proceed."

He exhales loudly.

"I had nothing to do with killing the woman in that cave. I'm pretty sure that was your precious Shaman Kyle. I found the body in there when I was scouting locations."

Plot twist. "Scouting locations for what?"

"Let's go, doll face. You're all out of second chances. Start walking toward that cave, or there's going to be two bodies up there — make it three."

If it were only my life, I'd probably roll the dice one more time. However, I can't take a risk on coming up snake eyes with someone else's life.

Turning, I keep my hands in the air and march back to the cave of petroglyphs and peril.

CHAPTER 18

ETHAN MAINTAINS HIS DISTANCE from us, but keeps his gun trained on our backs. He calls out instructions as we approach the cave.

When we reach the small plateau just outside the cave entrance, the Native American man sits down. "I will not enter the room of ancestors without a medicine man."

Ed waves his gun threateningly. "Then you can die out here." He raises the weapon and steadies his aim.

The only thing I can think of is money. I have no idea what motivates Ethan Vods, but in my limited experience with criminals, money is very near the top of most lists.

"How much money do you need, Ethan?"

The question catches him off guard and he

spins toward me, unconsciously lowering the gun. "Whaddya mean? Who've you been talking to? Who told you I needed money?"

My regular five senses, and a host of supporting psychic ones, all confirm I've chosen the right approach. "You don't strike me as a serial killer, Ethan. And people who aren't legit psychopaths generally kill out of desperation. I don't know what happened between you and Luminous Being, but killing me and this nice gentleman isn't going to make it better."

The man seated on the ground lifts a hand in greeting and smiles up at me. "My name is Peter Smith. But everyone around here calls me The Bag Man."

"Nice to meet you, Bag Man. I'm Mitzy Moon. Not from around here. I'm actually an incredibly wealthy heiress that lives in almost-Canada."

Wealthy and heiress hit home.

The gun hangs limply at Ethan's side. "How wealthy?"

"Tell you what, Ethan. Let this gentleman go, and I can guarantee you a ransom that will take care of any financial woes you're facing. How does that sound?" I feel a little like an infomercial hocking knives that cut through cans and tennis shoes, but I don't think the delivery matters. It's the promise of dollar bills that is pulling Ethan into my web.

"No way. Money first. Then I'll let him go." Ethan's narrow shoulders stiffen and his eyes flare with defiance.

Lowering my hands and taking a seat on a boulder near the entrance, I sigh heavily and shake my head. "Ethan, you strike me as an intelligent man. Even with my connections, it will take two or three days to get my hands on the cash. The longer you keep hostages up here, the more likely it is that you'll get caught. Let this guy go. He's not gonna say anything." I gesture to my fellow captor. "You're not gonna say anything, right, Bag Man?"

He leans back and shakes his head vigorously. "Say anything? What would I say? Who would I tell?"

Ethan rubs his smooth jaw with a smudged hand. His pale-green eyes dart left and then right. He's seriously considering my offer. "How do I know any of this is true? You're probably lyin' to me. People will say anything when they're faced with death."

"Is that so? Have you killed many people, Ethan? Did you kill Luminous Being?"

"Prove it." His lip curls into a snarl.

Ethan has jumped the train of the conversation and lost me. "Prove what? That you killed people?" This direction is making me nervous.

"No. Prove you can get the money. Call your bank."

Keeping my exterior calm, I let my insides go nuts. Call my bank! I can't even begin to imagine what Tilly Sikanen, sister to my favorite waitress, would say if I contacted her and demanded— "How much money do you need?"

Surprisingly, Ethan Vods runs his tongue along the inside of his left cheek and clearly does some mental calculations. "I need $300,000. Untraceable. Unmarked bills—"

Waving my hands, I roll my eyes. "Save me the speech. I'm not trying to set you up for a sting. I'm trying to save a man's life. If you let The Bag Man go, you'll get your money."

"Call your bank."

And here I am trapped in a *Catch* 22. Or maybe an image of a snake eating its own tail is more appropriate on this Native American land. Wait! Ethan doesn't know anyone at my bank. "No problem. I'll need my phone."

He retrieves my phone from his pack and places it in my clammy hand. "Put it on speaker."

A shift in the weather, or perhaps a special gift from the powers that be, grants me a signal.

The call is answered, and before my unbeknownst co-conspirator can speak, I toss out the deets. "Good afternoon. I need to speak to the man-

STIFFS AND PETROGLYPHS / 173

ager of the Pin Cherry Harbor Bank and Trust. Could you put Mr. Willoughby on please?"

There's a concerned harrumph, and my claircognizance takes a hit. Silas is definitely worried. "This is Mr. Willoughby."

"Oh, thank you for taking my call, sir. I'm sure you heard Erick and I are vacationing in the Southwest, and we've come across an amazing real estate opportunity. The only catch is, the realtor, Ethan Vods, says the owner of the property will only take cash."

Ethan grows agitated and waves the gun. He hisses, "Why'd you say my name?"

Silas Willoughby is no idiot, but I'm not sure he possesses the acting skills to pull this off.

"Mrs. Moon, how much would you be needing?"

"I will need $300,000 in cash, unmarked bills." Hopefully, the addition of that little nugget will confirm any suspicions Mr. Willoughby might have about the legitimacy of this deal.

"Indeed. It will take at least three days to handle a withdrawal of that size. Are we wiring the money to a local bank? We can't very well send cash via overnight courier."

Chuckling lightly, I glance at Ethan and shrug.

He's frantic. He paces the small flat dirt area

and waves the gun in the air. "Tell him we'll contact him later with the details."

"A wonderful question, sir. I hadn't considered those details, Mr. Willoughby. This is why I always tell you I'd never take my banking anywhere else." We share a chuckle, but I can hear the worry beneath his false bravado.

"Very well, Mrs. Moon. Once you've collected that information, please contact me directly and I'll make the arrangements. In the meantime, I shall inform your grandmother of your wonderful news. Oh, and I should mention Pyewacket loves the hematite necklace you sent him."

I greatly underestimated Silas. His acting skills are stellar, and he reminded me of a very special item in my possession.

"Wonderful. We should have that information in no time. I can't wait to tell Erick the good news when I find him."

Fingers crossed, my attempt at giving a reciprocal clue works as well.

"We'll speak soon, Mrs. Moon."

"Looking forward to it, Mr. Willoughby."

The call ends, and Ethan takes my phone. "You swear you'll get me the money?"

"I swear. If you let The Bag Man go, you'll have $300,000 as soon as humanly possible. Mr. Willoughby is old school. Taking care of his customers is number one. He would not disappoint me." It's strange how you can wrap the truth in a lie and create such a ring of authenticity.

Ethan turns to the man, aims the gun threateningly, and clears his throat. "I found you once. I can find you again. When I release you in the morning, go straight home and tell no one where you've been."

The Bag Man shifts, wrings his hands, and swallows hard. "I have a grandson. I am his caregiver. He needs special attention. Please release me. It's been hours since his bus—" Peter's voice catches in his throat, and I sense thick emotions swirling in his chest.

"Ethan, let him go tonight. If you wait until morning, the ransom drops to $250,000." It hardly seems like I'm in a position to negotiate, although the desperation rippling off Ethan would say otherwise.

He treads in a small circle, waves the gun, and exhales loudly. "Fine. Take off, Peter. But if I hear anything — and I mean anything — about what's going on at the retreat center, or what happened up here, you're a dead man."

Peter Smith quietly gets to his feet and begins his descent. When he reaches the bottom of the hill, he pauses, glances back at me and makes a strange gesture in the air.

It reminds me of the alchemical symbols Silas is always teaching. At first I dismiss it, but my extra senses are more diligent. It is a symbol of protection. A symbol handed down from his ancestors. The most precious gift he could offer me.

CHAPTER 19
ERICK

WHEN I ARRIVE BACK at camp with Officer Vincent, Kyle is in an inexplicable state of agitation.

He claims Two Trees has overdosed on psychedelic mushrooms, and he and Desert Flower could not restore the man to consciousness.

Officer Vincent examines Two Trees and immediately calls for an ambulance.

While he's on his radio, I examine Two Trees and note caked blood in his scruffy, light-brown dreadlocks.

Saying nothing, I glance toward the fire used to heat rocks for the sweat lodge and see cherry-red embers.

"Was there a second sweat today?"

There's definitely sweat on Kyle's upper lip. "It was a private sweat. Just for Rheegan."

"Oh, is she down by the creek?"

He shrugs. "How do I know?! I was taking care of Two Trees."

"And what about Desiree and Jonathan? Where are they?"

Kyle stops his pacing and clenches his jaw. "They left early. Desiree had a family emergency." His hands are balled into fists so tight his knuckles have whitened.

Desert Flower attempts to calm him with soothing words as she offers him water.

He slaps the cup from her hand, and she shrinks back in terror, as though reliving some previous abuse.

Officer Vincent returns with an update. "ETA on the ambulances is forty-five minutes."

"Forty-five minutes!" I throw my arms in the air.

He tilts his head. "This is not the big city, my friend."

"Sure. Sorry. Problem is, I don't think he's going to make it forty-five minutes. His breathing is shallow, and his pulse is already thready. It doesn't look good."

Officer Vincent takes my place beside the body, and I head toward the sweat lodge.

When I open the flap, a strange white cloud billows out. It's almost — cold. It rolls across the ground like fog, rather than rising and dissipating like steam.

Instinctively pulling my shirt up over my face, I duck into the sweat lodge to examine the rocks. There's plastic melted over several of them, creating an oddly unnatural sheen.

"Officer Vincent. I think you need to see this."

He stands, steps closer to the sweat lodge, and sniffs the air. "This is a disgrace."

"I'm sorry for how this disrespects your ancestors." Lowering my voice, I continue. "I suspect whatever happened to Two Trees was no accident. Did you notice the dried blood in his hair?"

Officer Vincent leans his head back and smiles knowingly. "You really were a lawman, Harper."

"When I opened the flap, a white cloud rolled out."

"Perhaps it was only thick steam. The steam may have been building for some time."

"It didn't behave like steam. It flowed low to the ground and almost felt cool. Then I found this." I gesture to the rocks.

Officer Vincent's demeanor changes in an instant.

"Let me see your food storage, Kyle."

At this point, Kyle is frenetic. He wouldn't look out of place in a 5150 lineup at my former station.

Desert Flower intervenes for her unhinged shaman. "It's over here, Officer."

She takes him to the large cooler in the shade beside the trailer.

After a thorough inspection, Officer Vincent returns. "Where's your dry ice?"

"My what? What are you saying? Dry ice? We don't use it. Only natural ice."

Vincent removes the handcuffs from his belt and steps toward Kyle. "You use dry ice. And you took that dry ice, and you threw it on the rocks in your sweat lodge. You profane the sacred and you have no remorse." He flicks the cuffs open. "Put your hands behind your back, Kyle."

Kyle snatches a large carving knife from the nearby prep station, lunges toward me, and holds the blade to my neck.

Officer Vincent hooks the cuffs back onto his duty belt and calmly pulls his gun. "Kyle, let Mr. Harper go. Adding another murder charge will not help you."

At that moment, I catch sight of the tip of the blade out of the corner of my eye. It's curving the wrong way. My breath catches in my throat and I can feel my heart racing. I have to remain calm. I can't show my hand. Kyle is pressing the dull side of the blade to my throat. I'm only gonna get one chance.

Vincent holds his weapon with steady assurance. In my heart, I know he's a good shot.

Taking a breath for courage, I elbow Kyle hard in the stomach, then grip his right wrist with both hands, spin away from him and smack his wrist on the prep table. The knife falls to the ground and I yank both of his arms behind his back.

Officer Vincent moves with the speed of a superhero. He closes the distance, tosses me the cuffs, and gives our perpetrator the standard speech about silence and attorneys.

Before I can truly celebrate our win, thoughts of my missing wife bubble to the surface.

"Where's Mitzy? If you help us out, Kyle, it could be the difference between first-degree murder charges, or involuntary manslaughter.

For a minute, I forgot my place. I glance toward officer Vincent, shrug my shoulders, and attempt an apologetic look.

Rather than a reprimand, he supports me. "That's right Kyle, if we find her alive—"

A call comes over his radio and interrupts whatever he was planning to say. "This is Vincent."

"Vincent, we got a call from Olive. She says she saw Lil' Sack wandering down the dirt road. The Bag Man didn't meet him."

I'm forgetting my manners all over the place in the commotion. "He left here almost two hours ago.

The Bag Man. He said he'd cut across the land to get there in time to meet his grandson."

Officer Vincent looks at me and shakes his head. Into the mic he commands, "Send Delshay to pick up Lil' Sack. And call Victorio in from standby. I need him over at this retreat center. I'm waiting for an ambulance. I've got a potential homicide, and there'll be a suspect in cuffs in the back of my car."

Vincent places Kyle in the back of the cruiser, parked in the shade of an old-growth oak. Kyle's chin drops to his chest and his eyes have a familiar vacant stare. When I was sheriff, I called it the look of guilt.

Then the officer tells Desert Flower to keep mopping Two Trees' head with cool water. From my vantage point, the drummer's chest is no longer moving, and I'm almost certain we've lost him. However, I admire the officer's attempt to keep the emotional woman busy.

He walks toward the rear of the cruiser and motions for me to follow.

"Where are we going?"

"You said your wife was looking around the land for a missing woman. Then you mentioned The Bag Man taking a shortcut. I feel these two things are the same. I feel it in my gut." He pats his stomach, looks at me, and nods solemnly.

I've never worked with law enforcement officers that openly admit to following intuition. It's like being surrounded by Mitzy at every turn. You'd think it would offer me comfort, but it only makes me worry about her more.

Vincent grabs flashlights, flares, and a large jug of water from the trunk of the cruiser before he locks it.

Initially, he leads the way toward the creek, but branches to the left and we move across open desert. The sun is warm, but as it lowers on the horizon, the intensity is diffused.

The desert is almost silent at this hour. It's as though the creatures know they have only a couple of hours to wait for the respite of the cool of night, and they're holding their breath.

The air is still and unusually dry. I never imagined I would miss something as simple as humidity. My lips are cracked and my eyes burn. "Can I have some water, Vincent?"

He hands me the jug. I take a short pull and wipe the top with my shirt before capping it. When I hand it back, he smiles.

"Afghanistan?"

I'd ask him how he knows, but I've seen enough men carefully meter out their water to know what tipped him off. "Two tours. You?"

"One tour for me. It's where I met my wife. She

wanted me to re-up, but when we found out she was pregnant, we both finished our contracts and came home. Tribal police were happy to have me. We have a good life here."

"You made the right choice, Vincent. You're doing a great job here, and I bet your wife is happy to have you around all the time."

He laughs. "I would not be so sure about that, Harper."

As we walk forward, my vision blurs. Blinking my eyes rapidly does nothing to clear the anomaly. Stopping, I rub my eyes in an attempt to get my bearings.

"You okay, Harper?"

"No. I can't see — or maybe I'm seeing too much."

He turns and looks at me. "What do you see?"

"There's the desert in front of me — but I see something else. It's like I'm dreaming, but I'm awake."

Officer Vincent drops the flares and the water, and grabs both of my shoulders. "Close your eyes, Harper. Forget where you are. Tell me what you see."

"Okay." His hands on my shoulders offer stability. Once I close my eyes, the confusing double vision ends and I feel like I'm watching a bad movie.

"It's like rocks. Like a rock wall. Wait . . .

There's something on the rock. Something scratched — pictures —"

"Petroglyphs?"

"Yeah. Yeah, I think they're petroglyphs."

As soon as I utter the word, the image vanishes.

"It's gone." Opening my eyes, I glance around and see nothing more than the darkening desert.

"Follow me, Harper. I know where that is."

I grab the flares, he grabs the water, and off we march. "You know where what is?"

"This wife of yours, is she special?"

It's not my secret to tell, but in the short time I've known Officer Vincent, I know I can trust him. "I think she's pretty special."

He chuckles. "The elders call it dreamwalking. There are many terms for it in the modern world. Have you heard of remote viewing?"

"Not ever."

Vincent inhales deeply. "Some people can share what they see with others. I think maybe your wife is someone like this. I think she is in the room of the ancestors. There are petroglyphs in that cave. Maybe she's injured and needs our help."

For some reason, this idea makes me laugh.

Vincent turns and looks at me in alarm.

"I'm not laughing about the injured part. But in my experience, it's a lot more likely that she's gotten herself into serious trouble with bad people. If we hadn't already caught Kyle, I'd assume he was holding her hostage."

Vincent slows his pace and motions for me to crouch behind him. His voice is barely a whisper. "I think you are near to the truth, Harper. Are you armed?"

"Yes, sir."

"That's the cave — up there. You approach from the front, and I will approach from behind. Let's get everyone out alive."

"Yes, sir."

He slips off the trail between prickly pear cactus, cat's claw, and all other sorts of thorny desert growth. I can see him with my eyes, but I hear nothing.

Attempting to follow his lead of stealth, I carefully continue down the trail with my best attempt at covert mode.

As I near the cave, Mitzy's voice flutters down like soft rain.

"Don't worry, Ethan. Mr. Willoughby at the bank will take care of everything. My grandmother was loaded."

A second voice — I'm assuming it must be Ethan — cuts through the air. "What do you mean, *was* loaded?"

There's a classic Mitzy pause. "What now?"

"What do you mean, *was* loaded? The guy from

the bank said he'd tell your grandmother about the house. What's going on?"

"I don't remember him saying that. Look, Ethan, you're under a lot of stress—"

There's a scuffle.

"There's no need to get the gun out, Ethan. No need at all. You'll get your money."

"I warned you about lying to me." The tone in her captor's voice is deadly serious.

Keep runnin' that beautiful mouth of yours, Mitzy. I'm almost there.

CHAPTER 20

I MAY HAVE GOTTEN Peter Smith a.k.a. The Bag Man safely out of this cave, but things have taken an ugly turn. It would appear I'm about to meet Peter's ancestors — with or without a medicine man.

The sharp howl of a coyote throws Ethan off his game. He really should've thought about taping my feet back together when he re-taped my wrists.

One swift kick from my left leg and I can almost hear the mantra from *Karate Kid*. "Sweep the leg. Sweep the leg."

Ethan Vods goes down hard, and the gun is knocked loose from his hand. I scramble toward the pistol, but a steel grip encircles my ankle.

Ethan tugs.

I kick my free leg wildly, and he shouts in pain. Temporary satisfaction floods through me. Using my elbows to drag myself forward, I'm nearly within reach of the gun.

Angry hands claw at both of my ankles and drag me backward across the cave floor.

I'm down to my last move — a Kwai Chang Caine special. I grab some dirt in my hands and envision myself twisting and flinging the dirt into my attacker's eyes.

I'm young. I'm not necessarily athletic. The move resembles that of a lumbering seal attempting to climb over a rocky beach, and the toss of dirt is ruled by the all-too-real influence of gravity.

My eyes are filled with dust, my wrists are taped together, and all I can imagine is dying without getting to say goodbye to my amazing—

"Drop the gun, or I'll drop you."

It may as well be the voice of an angel. "Erick! You got my message."

Rocks cascade over the cave entrance and a second pair of feet hit the ground beside my brave husband.

My eyes are watering. A combination of tears of joy and my body's natural desire to flush the cave dirt.

The Native American man in uniform grabs his handcuffs and exchanges a look with Erick.

I attempt to keep my composure with some signature snark. "Hey, honey, who's your friend?"

Once Ethan is under control, Erick holsters his gun and rushes forward. He scoops me into his arms and uses his T-shirt to wipe the tearstains from my face.

"Oh, that's Vincent. He's one of your people."

Tilting my head and staring at the handsome Yavapai-Apache officer, I shake my head in confusion. "As far as I know, I don't have any Native American ancestors."

Erick pulls me close, kisses my cheek, and whispers, "He's got more intuition than your average human, if you know what I mean."

Ignoring my trembling hands, I melt into the arms of my husband and peek over his shoulder at Officer Vincent. "Thanks for following your *hunches*, Vincent. I was trying to buy my way out of this situation with a ransom payment. Maybe you can think of something I could do with that money for the Yavapai-Apache nation, to show them my gratitude. I mean, you literally saved my life."

Vincent pushes his prisoner toward the cave mouth, looks over his shoulder, and smiles warmly. "The elders are meeting tonight. I will pass along your generous offer to The Bag Man, once we find him. He always has business with them."

"Thanks. He's safe. The Bag Man left here less than an hour ago. I bought his freedom, so he could get back to his grandson."

Ethan scoffs and grumbles under his breath.

Ignoring him, I update my rescuers. "Oh, and I hate to spoil this reunion with more bad news, but the body of Luminous Being is near the back of the cave. This guy claims he didn't put her in here, but if you don't mind, I'd like to ask him a couple of questions."

Erick removes the last of the tape from my wrists and helps me to my feet. I rub at the red itchy blotches on my skin and walk toward Ethan Vods. Reaching into my backpack, I remove the hematite necklace Silas mentioned and hang it around my neck.

Officer Vincent glances at the stone, smiles briefly, and rakes a hand through his obsidian black hair. "Ask away, Mrs. Harper."

"It's Mrs. Moon. But I'll answer to Mrs. Harper." I toss a wink at Erick and step around to face Ethan. "Ethan Vods, did you kill Luminous Being?"

"No. And I didn't kill Greta Neff either." Ethan's posture is rigid.

"Greta Neff?"

"That's her actual name." He swallows twice.

"Noted. Keep talking. Why is she dead, Ethan? And why do you know her given name?"

The tendons in his neck protrude as he struggles against the power of the necklace, but in the end he is compelled to spill his guts.

"She had an affair with Kyle's father. Remiel established a large commune in New Mexico. I was his right-hand man. I handled all the recruiting events and managed the day-to-day. People would surrender all their wealth to him for the chance at a place in his celestial realm. Kyle was Remiel's oldest son, and Kyle's mother held special status due to her gift to the community. One day, Greta showed up and Remiel offered her the reward of a private ascension."

My eyes widen, and Erick shakes his head in disgust.

"Anyway, Remiel became obsessed with the chick. Then Greta's sister died in a car crash and she suddenly couldn't take the commune life. By that time, she'd weaseled her way into more than his bed. She emptied our bank accounts and disappeared. Changing her name was just part of her plan to hide from me."

Wow! This truth necklace is magnificent. I may have to wear it more often. "So you just happened to show up in a random cave in the middle of Arizona where *someone else* dumped her dead body?"

"Yeah. Sort of." He shifts his weight. "She stole the money and vanished. I picked up her trail in Colorado, followed her to Utah, almost caught her in Las Vegas, and then wound up in Phoenix." He twists his wrists in the cuffs and looks absently at the petroglyphs.

"Why would you kill her?"

Ethan exhales loudly. "I didn't kill her. I was trying to find her, so I could get the money back. I thought it would help Kyle get back on his feet. When she disappeared, Remiel lost faith. He gathered his inner circle in an exclusive sweat lodge and killed them all, including himself, by throwing several chunks of dry ice on the hot stones."

Erick inhales sharply and exchanges a look with Officer Vincent.

I feel like the wallflower at the dance. "And?"

Ethan exhales and shakes his head. "The dry ice instantly sublimates to CO_2 gas and replaces oxygen in the bloodstream. In an enclosed space . . . They died quickly. At least that's what the coroner told us." He shrugs and his gaze drops to the dirt floor. "After that, the commune disbanded. Kyle hasn't seen his mother since."

We nod, but his story still seems a little thin. "So, back to ending up in this cave—"

"I knew Kyle could run his own center. He'd learned at his father's feet for years. But he was broken and disillusioned. He disappeared. When I ran into him in Phoenix, he was leading some kind of group meditation and people seemed to worship him. I convinced him that the best way to honor his father would be to set up his own retreat center, and told him we could get a piece of Native land. The tie-in with the Native American community would legitimize his whole operation."

Erick pipes up. "And he bought that?"

Ethan turns, scowls, and looks back at the stone dangling around my neck. "Everything was going great. Then that Bag Man guy started poking around and discovered Kyle wasn't keeping up his end of the 'spiritual contract.'" He clenches his jaw and continues. "There's no controlling Kyle. Once he had the sojourners filling up the retreat center, it became apparent he'd inherited his father's narcissism. He wouldn't listen to reason. Kyle started to think he *was* an archangel. I had to get rid of our earthly problem — the guy who was going to complain — so I scouted the area, looking for a place to hide a body. I know how to make things look like an accident. Just needed the perfect location."

Erick grumbles. It doesn't take a psychic to know that he's thinking there's no perfect location for a murder.

"I was in the cottonwoods along the creek and saw that Two Weeds, or whatever that loser druggie's name is, carrying a big sleeping bag over his shoulder. Looked suspicious, so I followed him."

Rubbing the necklace with my right hand, I prompt Ethan. "And where did he go?"

"He was high out of his mind. Singing all the way up the hill. He disappeared into the cave with whatever he was carrying. When he came out, the sleeping bag was empty. He headed straight back to camp. So I checked into it."

Erick catches my eye and arches an eyebrow. I tap the necklace and he grins. Seems we agree that this Ethan Vods is diabolical. "And what did you find?"

"I recognized Greta right away."

"You mean Luminous Being." I place a hand on my hip and exhale.

"Yeah. Whatever. Anyway, I couldn't believe that drum-beating idiot had actually killed Greta."

"So you were telling the truth when you said you didn't put the body up here?"

"Yeah. And I am telling the truth now. I didn't kill her. Kyle was supposed to confront her. Find out about the money she stole. Get closure."

A little spark tickles my brain. "So you somehow got Greta to come to this retreat. How?"

"I saw that outrageous painting in the coffee shop and left some brochures on the counter. She'd fallen for the woo woo song and dance once. I figured she could fall again."

"Wouldn't she recognize Kyle?"

"Nah, that was almost ten years ago. Kyle was

eighteen, had a shaved head, and was lost in Remiel's shadow."

"So instead of closure, Kyle recognized her and killed her?"

"No way Kyle did this. He's too clever. But maybe he said something to make his boy kill the chick. Two Weeds—"

"Two Trees." Man, this guy annoys me.

"Yeah. He worshipped the shaman. Claimed he'd had some cosmic breakthrough because of Kyle's connection to the angels. In reality, Kyle kept him set up with weed and psychedelic mushrooms. That guy would do anything for him."

Officer Vincent glances around Ethan's shoulder and nods. "I need to get the suspect back to our station, Mrs. Moon. Your husband knows where it is. Come by and make a statement when you can, okay?"

"Of course." I can't help but compare Vincent's easy, relaxed manner with the tightly wound bully Sheriff Paulsen back home. Sure was nice to work a case without her breathing down our necks.

Vincent marches Ethan Vods out of the cave, and Erick joins me on the small plateau outside the entrance.

The sun has almost slipped away. Thin wispy clouds stretch across the sky like cotton candy threads that catch the last glow of orange, pink, and indigo. Coolness drifts through the parched land.

A coyote howls, and another answers the call.

Officer Vincent shouts from the darkening desert floor. "Coyote has avenged Greta's death."

Erick slips his arm around my waist, and I lean into him, exhausted from my ordeal.

CHAPTER 21

I HAD FORGOTTEN the magical feeling of a full moon over the desert. As Erick and I walk back to camp, it could almost be midday. The orb in the sky is so silver-bright, we can see our shadows crisp against the trail as we walk.

"Hey, how did you find me?"

He pulls me tighter and I can feel cords of worry still woven around his body. "It's hard to explain. I was walking with Officer Vincent and all of a sudden I couldn't see what was in front of me."

My heartbeat quickens. "What did you see?"

"I think I was seeing the drawings on the wall outside that cave where we found you. Do you think I'm psychic now?" His expression is deeply serious.

Stopping in the moonlight, I hug him tightly,

slip my arms around his neck, and kiss his full pouty mouth "No. But I think you're incredibly open-minded and brilliant."

He chuckles. "What did you do?" Erick's eyes shimmer with love as he gazes down at me and I explain the process of sending an image telepathically. "Silas told me it's like attaching a file to an email. Only it's a mental picture. Make sense?"

My kind-hearted husband shrugs as though it's no big deal. "Oh, that. Yeah, it's called remote viewing."

Playfully punching him in the chest, I chuckle as I reply. "Oh, remote viewing? So you're some kind of extrasensory perception expert now, are you?"

"Not in the least. I'm just messing with you, Moon. Officer Vincent was the one who knew what was happening. I told you he was one of your people."

We resume our trek toward camp and, as the calming moonlight fills me, my super-sleuth genes kick into overdrive. "Hey, how did you get Kyle to come clean about what was going on?"

Erick rolls his head back and forth on his shoulders and groans. "Right. I completely forgot that you weren't aware of the second murder."

Screeching to a halt, I toss my fist on my hip. "The what now?"

He steps back and gesticulates wildly as he tells the unbelievable tale of Two Trees' murder.

"Mind blown, Harper. Mind Blown." Rubbing my hands together, I process this new info. "So, Kyle learned this dastardly trick from his father and killed Luminous Being and Two Trees?"

Erick shakes his head. "Vincent wasn't a hundred percent sure. He's waiting for all the facts to be evaluated, but it definitely seemed like Two Trees was some kind of minion. Plus, that Ethan guy sure seemed convinced it was the drummer who killed her. The evidence and testimonies will probably show that Two Trees killed Luminous Being to protect his shaman, and then Kyle returned the favor by killing Two Trees before he could spill the beans."

"Wow! Two murders and two different killers. I think that's a new record for us, Harper."

He grabs my hand and shakes his head. "And I hope it's a record we never break."

"Copy that."

The moon seems to follow us like a gentle protector as we continue our journey, but I can't help worrying about The Bag Man's grandson. "Do you think The Bag Man got back in time to help his grandson? I felt terrible about that. I was willing to offer anything to get that man his freedom."

"That's what I'm always afraid of." Erick

squeezes my hand hard. "Fortunately, there's good news on that front. Someone called in to the station to report seeing Lil' Sack wandering the road, and Officer Vincent sent one of his guys out to pick the boy up. Sounded like everything was going to be fine. Once again, I have to say, it was foolishly brave of you to sacrifice yourself for someone you hardly knew."

"Was it? I guess I didn't really think about it at the time. I just knew there was someone in danger and that I might be able to help. I have a real problem, Harper. Do you think there's a twelve-step program for hero syndrome?"

He pulls his hand from mine, slips an arm around my waist, and squeezes me. "I hope not. Like I always say, I love you exactly the way you are."

The cool night air weaves its way around us, and the burbling water of the creek seems to whisper, "It's all over. Some were saved."

"I'm really not looking forward to breaking this news to Dean."

Erick nods and kisses the top of my head. "Yeah. He seemed pretty in love with the woman. What about all that money she stole from Remiel? Thoughts?"

"Good question. If we find the money, we could

use it to compensate the Yavapai-Apache tribe for Kyle running his scheme on their land."

Erick rubs his fingers on my arm as he takes a deep, thoughtful breath. "True. Although, even though it was stolen from a fraudulent self-appointed messiah, it's still stolen money."

"Hey, don't break your brain, Harper. The money is ill-gotten gains. There would be no way to return it to the people Remiel defrauded. The best thing would be to use it to do good."

"Maybe. That's assuming it's ever found."

"Um, psychic extraordinaire here." I stop and take an unnecessary bow.

He laughs. "Begging your pardon, Your Highness. Let's talk to Dean first, and see what he knows about Greta's past, and maybe give the matter a day or two while we see the sights in Sedona. Plus, you promised to take me to the Grand Canyon this time."

"All right, tourist boy. We'll talk to Dean tomorrow. Then we can see what his info leads to in the next couple of days, and if all else fails we'll leave it to the authorities. But I want to do something for the Yavapai-Apache people, even if we don't find the stolen money. Maybe they could use another bus or some scholarships at their school."

Erick rubs my shoulder. "I think they could use some new patrol cars and some quads, or maybe rail buggies. They have a lot of rough country to patrol, and Vincent said all they have besides their vintage cruisers are a couple of horses on their actual last legs."

The idea of helping lifts my spirits and temporarily moves my thoughts away from the murders.

"I love all those ideas. Let's do everything. I think it would be absolutely wonderful to give them an upgrade. We can talk to The Bag Man about why the bus doesn't drop his grandson off closer to home. Maybe there's a solution there, too."

We arrive at camp, and Erick unzips the door to our yurt. "One more night in this contraption, and then you can save the world. Sound good?"

"Which part? The saving the world or one more night in this flimsy old tent sleeping next to *you*?" I waggle my eyebrows in case he's not picking up what I'm laying down.

He zips the door closed behind us and kisses me with serious intentions. "Keep talking like that, Moon, and you'll be lucky to get any sleep at all."

Bluff called!

WE COULD HAVE BAILED on the bogus retreat last night, but Winter and Ivan seem like good people who we may actually invite to Pin Cherry Harbor. Sticking around for one last breakfast with the gang is the most grown-up thing to do. And Erick Harper is nothing if not grown-up.

Skipping the mush they call oatmeal, I load up on fruit and gluten-free English muffins.

Now that our shady shamanic ruler has been removed in handcuffs, breakfast is rule free. We all crowd around a single table, and Desert Flower brings her mug of tea and slides onto the bench beside Ivan.

I smile and offer a welcoming head nod.

She lifts her mug in a silent toast before drinking deeply.

"If you have any information for the tribal police, it would be great if you'd stop off and give a statement as you leave the land." Erick smiles pleasantly at each of the remaining sojourners and drinks his boiled-twig tea like a pro.

Rheegan keeps her gaze fixed on her bowl and stirs her spoon aimlessly in a clockwise motion.

Desert Flower rubs the rose quartz dangling around her neck and pipes up. "You know, I heard Shaman Kyle arguing with Luminous about money, but I thought it was about package prices or something. I had no idea she was the vixen who destroyed Shaman Kyle's family."

I've reached the end of my new-age macramé rope. "Desert Flower, I know your heart is in the right place, but Kyle was no more a shaman than

Erick is a yeti. You need to let this all go and move on with your life. Hopefully, you'll find someone more authentic and trustworthy in your next venture."

Desert Flower bites her bottom lip, but it's Rheegan who bursts into tears.

Erick furrows his brow at me and shakes his head.

Apparently, I picked the wrong moment for radical honesty.

Sliding off the bench, I walk around the table and put an arm around Rheegan. "Hey, I'm sorry if I hurt your feelings. You didn't do anything wrong. I'm upset with Kyle, and the way he fleeced every-one. But it's definitely not your fault."

She sniffles and wipes her nose with the back of her hand. "He — said — he — loved me." Tears spill from her eyes, and she clings to me like Kate Winslet clung to that floating door in the Atlantic. As I pat her back and mumble a series of there, theres, Winter offers his take.

"I think we should be incredibly proud of what we've done here. We all worked together to solve two murders and made lifelong friends, too!" He claps his hands together and throws an arm around Ivan's shoulders.

Erick smiles. "That's right. The experiences that you each had aren't invalidated because Kyle's heart wasn't in the right place. You can only control yourself. And if your heart was holding the right intention, then you got what you needed out of this retreat."

My tendency toward humor as a coping mechanism is rolling like a freight train down a mountain. I don't want to say it — but I can't stop it. "Everyone, may I introduce Shaman Erick."

Thankfully, my irreverence does the trick, and all the sojourners, including Rheegan, laugh conspiratorially.

Desert Flower gets to her feet and waits for all eyes to turn toward her. "I don't know how quickly the police will freeze the accounts, but I plan to refund all of your money immediately, if I can. I'm so sorry about all of this. I only ever agreed to work with him because I believed he truly wanted people to follow their bliss and find their passion."

Everyone claps for her, and Ivan gets to his feet. "I'm sure everyone appreciates that, Desert Flower. Like Erick said, Shaman Kyle may not have been what he appeared to be, but we all got what we needed from this retreat. So if the accounts are frozen and you can't refund—"

Winter jumps up and playfully throws a hand over Ivan's mouth. "Hush! Do you know how many cute sweaters I could buy for Poco with that money?"

Another round of laughter draws us together in a survivors' bond.

All that's left is to drive into town and break the terrible news to Dean.

And, I did promise Erick we'd spend a couple days trying to track down the stolen—

"It's a key!"

All the heads whip pan toward me, and I cover my red-cheeked face with my hands.

CHAPTER 22

MAKING DECIDEDLY LAME EXCUSES for my key-
related outburst, I get to my feet and grin stupidly.
"Erick, I'm gonna run back and pack our things.
Winter and Ivan already know the truth. You may
as well fill in Rheegan. Then we need to go see
Dean."

Erick glances up and, despite the smirk on his
face, his eyes are filled with love. "10-4."

I race to our tent thing-y and recover the small
cloth-wrapped package I found under the bed
when I searched Luminous Being's yurt.

To my great pleasure, it is a key. To what? I have
no idea, and neither my extra senses nor my tem-
peramental mood ring offer any clues. I shove the
bundle in my pocket and shrug.

Time to pack the suitcases. Remarkably few

items have actually been removed. When I retrieve Erick's gun case from its hiding place, it feels unusually light. My psychic abilities and my common sense confirm he's packing heat and I'm packing an empty gun case.

After everything that transpired in the last couple of days, I can hardly blame him for keeping the gun on his person.

Uh oh! The Scooby Gang is going to have my hide. Erick seriously distracted me from making any phone calls last night, and hunger compelled me to the outdoor eating area without a single thought of Grams and Pye. Better patch this hole ASAP!

"Good morning, Pye—"

"Mizithra Achelois Moon! What on earth is going on out there? Mr. Cuddlekins and I didn't get a wink of sleep." Grams flits back and forth behind the stoic caracal and her glow flickers like a dying candle.

I'll skip reminding her that ghosts don't sleep and get straight to the apology. "I'm truly sorry, Grams. I was too exhausted to call last night — plus, there probably wasn't any reception. It seems to get worse at night." I paint my features in the portrait of innocence and protect Erick's role in my *forgetfulness*.

Pyewacket blinks once, but makes no sound.

Grams pushes through him, creating a glowing

Ghost-ma halo around my caracal. The effect is eerie and unsettling. "And this morning?"

Gulp. "I was hungry?" My mouth feels dry.

"Are you asking me or telling me, young lady?" She withdraws and Pye seems to grin.

"All right, you two. Enough scolding. Do you want to hear about how I found the body, got kid-napped, rescued The Bag Man, and solved the second murder — or not?"

"Reow." Can confirm.

"Oh, my goodness. Spill!" Grams claps her hands together as though they're castanets.

As I unfold the story of Ethan, Kyle, Two Trees, Greta, and Remiel, I take creative license where necessary. I haven't heard Kyle's confession yet, but if we get to the tribal police station in time, I'm bet-ting my assumptions won't be far from the truth.

"I'm not at all happy with the risks you're taking out there, dear. When do you get home?" Grams taps a perfectly manicured finger on her coral lip.

"Hey, we solved two murders and broke up a spiritual scam." I attempt to scowl, but I'm so happy to be alive and chatting with my besties that I can't hold the face. "We'll be home soon. I promised to show Erick the sights, and then we'll hit the road — I mean, skies."

"Whenever it is, it won't be soon enough." Grams blows me an ethereal kiss.

"Do you miss me too, Pye?"

"Ree-ow." Soft but condescending.

"I'll take it." Blowing kisses back, I end the call and close the suitcases.

Returning to the eating area, only Erick and Desert Flower remain seated at the wooden table.

"Did you scare everyone off, Harper?"

"Nah. They took the PI news in stride. Everyone went to finish packing. I offered Desert Flower a lift to the tribal police headquarters. All future retreat reservations have been canceled, and she was able to refund everyone's money — for this most recent trip. It seems Kyle was funneling money out of that account into a private account she can't access."

Smiling at Desert Flower, as she adjusts her tie-dyed head wrap, I offer the only thing I have. "Hey, I know your heart was in the right place. Kyle was definitely charismatic. I hope you won't let one bad apple spoil your desire to help others. It's hard to overcome a betrayal like that."

I'm sure her reply is bright and hopeful, but all I can think of is my golden-eyed, furry overlord appearing in my dreams and whispering that word. *Betrayal*. Luminous Being betrayed Remiel. Two Trees betrayed Luminous Being, and Kyle betrayed Two Trees. What a twisted circle.

"All right, Erick. Let's hit the road."

Winter jogs up the path, waving recklessly. "Hey, hang on a minute!"

He pauses beside Erick and smiles. "Ivan and I wanted to invite ourselves to Pin Cherry Place? What is it called?"

Erick chuckles. "Pin Cherry Harbor. You're both welcome anytime. Thanks for keeping our secret while we solved this case. I hope the next time we all get together, it will be under decidedly better circumstances."

Winter flashes his perfect white teeth. "Oh, for sure. We absolutely look forward to spending some non-murder-y time with the two of you!"

With that, he hugs us each in turn.

"Give our best to Ivan. We'll see you when we see you." I wave and shrug.

He offers one final wave and races off toward the yurts.

Erick glances at my empty hands. "I thought you said you were going to pack us up?"

"Look, Harper. You're the one who's always saying we play to our strengths. I'm an expert at packing a suitcase, and your strength is lugging it around. Everything's ready and waiting in the yurt. Including your empty gun case."

His big blue eyes widen and he snickers. "Yeah, I don't think I'm going to feel a hundred percent safe until we're at the airport."

Erick repeats his invite to give Desert Flower a lift to the tribal police station.

She accepts and we all pile into the Jeep.

The bumpy ride down the dirt road feels like the ending of a movie, but I know it's only the beginning of many new decisions for Desert Flower.

Erick parks in front of the station, jogs around, and opens our doors. Inside, Officer Vincent is taking Kyle's statement.

Unlike the Pin Cherry Harbor Sheriff's station, this one-room building, with a single holding cell at the back, has no private interrogation rooms.

This will be the easiest eavesdropping I've ever done!

Officer Vincent takes notes long hand. "Kyle. Can you tell me what happened to your father, Remiel?"

A sheen of sweat glistens above his lip, but he basically echoes what Ethan Vods told us in the room of the ancestors.

Officer Vincent glances at his notepad and back toward Kyle. "Why did you invite Greta Neff to your retreat center?"

Kyle attempts to throw his arms in the air, but since his wrists are handcuffed together, it becomes an empty gesture. "For the third time, I didn't invite her. Ethan said he put brochures around town. She probably saw one of them and was drawn like a moth to a flame."

"Can you explain?"

"Explain? I thought you said Ethan told you all about how she was in my dad's commune. She's a guru groupie. Do I really have to repeat it?"

"I'd like you to tell me in your own words." Officer Vincent makes a note on the paper and waits with a level of patience I could never dream of achieving.

Kyle glances around the modest station and swallows before condescending to respond. "Fine. I was a teenager. Blindly following my narcissistic father. He actually thought he was the Savior. Why not? People followed him around, worshiped at his feet, gave him everything they had — and for what? He never fulfilled his promises. He just kept making more. My mother praised and defended him to the bitter end. He slept with all the women in the commune. I have more half-brothers and half-sisters than a bunch of inbred—"

"That's enough. Stick to the facts, please. How did Greta destroy your family, as you claim?"

"As I claim? It's not a claim. It's a fact. She came in. She wormed her way into my father's bed. And within months, she was working late in his makeshift office and apparently had access to every bank account he'd ever opened. Not that there was that much in any of them. Ethan was always selling things off, investing in the land, covering our tracks, and a bunch of other euphemisms for embezzling."

"If you had such a strong dislike for Mr. Vods, why did you continue to work with him?"

Kyle tilts his head back, and an exasperated sigh escapes. "I tried to get away. After my dad killed himself, I didn't believe in anything. I took off and worked odd jobs for cash. I got into meditation as a goof. But, you know, it kinda helped. It calmed me down. It took away some of the anger." He lifts his manacled hands and scratches his chin. "When I ran into Ethan in that coffee shop in Phoenix, I bought what he was selling. He's a slick talker. That's why my dad always had him in charge of re-cruiting. He could sell coffins to the cremated, you know?"

Officer Vincent nods as he consults his list. However, my inner snoop has a bad case of the blurts.

"Did Greta recognize you when she arrived at the retreat?"

Kyle glances angrily at me, but Officer Vincent nods for him to answer.

"No. She never even looked at me back at the commune in New Mexico. But I have a lot of my father's mannerisms. Used some of his parables. It took her a day to make the connection, and once she did — that's when the arguing started."

"So you recognized her right away?" I move my chair closer and invite myself to the interrogation.

"Of course. Those stupid blonde braids. Whatever! Even with a new hairdo, I would've recognized those deceitful eyes. I demanded that she repay the money she stole and threatened to turn her over to the authorities for killing my father."

Officer Vincent drops his pen to the table. "I thought your father committed suicide? Are you saying Greta Neff is responsible for murder?"

Kyle leans back and puffs up his chest. "She might as well be. She destroyed him. When she stole that money and disappeared, he was unmoored. He turned his back on everything he believed in. He had no reason to remain on this earth. At least that's what it said in the note he left my mother." His jaw muscles tighten. "My mom took one look at that note, grabbed her satchel, and left me and the land behind. I became an orphan that day." The emotions that grip Kyle's features are quite real. My extrasensory perception confirms that his father's death was catastrophic for him, and the taillights from my earlier vision must've been the memory of his mother leaving.

"I'm sorry about your father, Kyle. My mother died when I was eleven. I know it's not easy."

He glances at me, but instead of understanding or acknowledgment, it feels as though his gaze drips venom. "Everyone thinks they understand. They don't. When your father makes you believe he's an Archangel of God himself—" An angry tear leaks from the corner of his eye and he swipes it fiercely away.

"Kyle, did you kill Greta Neff?" My psychic senses offer no clue to his answer.

"No. Like I said, that pothead Two Trees must've misunderstood something I said. I got kind of wasted one night and blurted out what she'd done to my family. I was really angry. He misunderstood, okay?"

As I'm about to open my mouth with a follow-up question, the slow and steady voice of Erick Harper silences me. "And who knocked Two Trees unconscious and dragged him into the sweat lodge to be killed by the dry ice, Kyle?"

Officer Vincent gazes expectantly at his suspect.

Kyle lays his handcuffed arms on the table and drops his head with a heavy exhale. "I want a lawyer. You can't prove anything. I want a lawyer. Where's Ethan?"

Officer Vincent glances toward the holding cell. "Mr. Vods is in the cell, as you know. The fingerprints at the scene of Two Trees' murder will certainly match yours. A confession would go a long way toward leniency, Kyle. Any jury is going to be moved by genuine remorse."

Kyle's head slowly rises from the table, and his eyes are as black as coal. His voice, only a gravelly whisper, seems to fill the room with hate. "Remorse? I have no remorse."

Officer Vincent's shoulders slump, and I sense his disappointment.

I wish I could tell him about the key, but I have no idea if it will lead anywhere. Best if I keep my lips sealed, for now.

Erick takes me by the hand and pulls my chair back to the small table where he and Desert Flower are seated.

The young lawman calmly places his pen on his pad, grips Kyle by the right arm, and returns him to the holding cell without a word.

Creepy vengeful fake shaman! I seriously cannot wait to get out of here.

Vincent returns and pulls a chair up next to Erick. "You three want to write down your statements for me?"

Erick nods and takes the pad and pen from Vincent.

I'm a little less inclined to do homework. "Can I tell Erick, and have him write it down for me?"

Vincent laughs openly. "Sure. I know he's got experience."

A smirk creeps across my face. "And he's got very nice penmanship."

The three of us share a hollow chuckle while Erick and Desert Flower write up their statements. Once my hubby finishes with his, I give him an extremely abbreviated version of my experience in the cave, and sign the statement when he's done.

Erick approaches Officer Vincent's desk and hands him the notepads. "Thanks again for your help out there. Mitzy and I are very grateful for the rescue. She's got some good ideas for ways to thank the tribe. When we get back to Pin Cherry Harbor, she'll speak to her attorney about making that all happen."

Vincent gets to his feet, shakes Erick's hand, and smiles. "It was good to work with you. I wish you and your wife the best with your private investigator's business."

Joining Erick, I add my thanks.

After returning Desert Flower to her camper, we head off the land.

I'm not looking forward to dealing with Dean, but hopefully his super-positive attitude will allow him to move on more quickly than most.

CHAPTER 23

ONCE DESERT FLOWER releases us from her repeated hugs, we pile into the car and head out. As we reach the paved road my phone pings like a pinball machine on crack!

More missed calls from my furry overlord!

"Can you pull over while I have signal? If I don't call Grams, she might force Pye to contact the National Guard."

We chuckle, but Erick knows I'm right. He pulls onto the shoulder and I prepare for the worst.

"Hey, Grams. Where's Pyewacket?"

"Oh, he skulked out of here after your call and I haven't seen him since. It pains him to admit how much he misses you."

"I miss him like crazy too. When he shows up,

be sure to tell him he was right about everything! As per usual."

Grams widens her shimmering eyes and floats closer to the screen. Whatever she says is garbled by her ghostly energy interfering with the Phoom connection.

"Grams! Back up. The screen's going all ba-jiggity."

A moment later, the image returns to normal, and I hear the end of her speech.

". . . and I will not stand for it in the future."

I know better than to pull that thread. "All right. We'll see you soon."

"Hold on, young lady. You didn't give me an update. I need the final wrap up. How is a ghost to survive on such little information?"

"Begging your pardon, Your Spectral Highness." We share a chuckle and I continue. "It was a double murder, as I mentioned, but definitely with two separate killers. Former shaman Kyle wouldn't confess, but there's enough evidence without that. We're going to talk to Dean right now and break the bad news about Luminous Being a.k.a. Greta Neff. Then I'm taking Erick to the Grand Canyon and we may have one last loose end to tie up, but I'll fill you in completely when we get back to town."

"Well, that's not much to go on, Mizithra. I suppose it will have to do. I'll leave the murder board

right where it is until you walk me through the details, step by step."

"Can't wait." Proudly, I suppress my eye roll.
"Hey, how's your energy? Are you still feeling
drained?"

"Silas and I had a little chat, well, with the 3 x 5
cards and his alchemically altered eyeglasses. He
thinks all my work on the memoirs is wearing me
out." She sighs dramatically.

"It's fine by me if you abandon the project,
Grams." It's difficult to suppress my giggle.

"Oh, you'd love that, wouldn't you, dear?"

"I only have your best interests at heart, Isadora.
You know, just like when you talk me into designer
dresses and five-inch heels." We share a chuckle.
"Did he have any suggestions?"

"You know Silas. He has to do some research,
read a stack of tomes, and then he'll have some options. Don't worry about me. Just get yourself and
your charming husband safely back to Pin
Cherry."

"Copy that."

"I love you, sweetie."

"I love you too, Grams."

Erick leans toward the camera and adds, "I love
you too, Grams-in-Law."

She flutters her eyelashes and pats her chest as
though she can't catch her breath. Regardless of the

fact that ghosts don't breathe. "Oh, Mitzy, that man is such a keeper."

"Don't I know it. Bye, Grams."

Erick pulls onto the highway and drives straight to the Brewed Dog. Riding beside him in silence, I'm filled with an equal mixture of dread and empathy.

Deep breath.

Dean catches my eye the second we walk through the door.

I nod to the chairs in the back and head toward them without placing an order.

He hurries after us, in his cargo shorts and company branded T-shirt. His man bun is messy and hanging low against the back of his neck. And the bags under his eyes are new.

He takes a seat and leans toward me expectantly.

"Dean, I've been where you are. I'm not gonna pull any punches or use any clever euphemisms. Luminous Being is dead. I'm sorry to have to tell you, it was not accidental. All we found was her phone and a key. I don't know what happened to the rest of her belongings."

Tears trickle down his cheeks and disappear into his goatee. All the hope he'd been holding in his heart pours out in one mournful exhale. "I knew it. I felt it. I should've done more right away."

"You can't blame yourself, Dean. Like I said. I've been exactly where you are now. There's nothing that you could have done. Luminous Being, or as she was known before she came here, Greta Neff, lead a dangerous life. She stole close to a hundred thousand dollars from a cult leader named Remiel, and his right-hand guy has been chasing her across state after state."

"A cult leader killed her?" Dean seems more confused than I would've thought.

"How much did you know about her life before she came here?"

He looks at the bamboo flooring and shrugs. "Not much. Nothing really. We agreed not to bring old baggage into this relationship."

"I know you probably thought that was for the best, but I don't think Greta agreed to those terms for the right reasons. She was hiding — hiding herself and hiding a ton of money."

Dean lifts his head. "She had money? Luminous always acted like she could barely make ends meet. She had to borrow money from me a couple of times."

"Hey, I'm not going to speak ill of the dead, but usually a leopard can't change its spots."

Dean crosses his arms and leans back. "Should I try to contact her family?"

"You can probably leave that to the authorities,

Dean. I realize you may still be holding onto a fantasy of what she was, but I think it'll help you heal if you can let that go."

He nods, bites his bottom lip, and wipes an errant tear from his cheek. "I super appreciate you coming out here to help me. What do I owe you guys?"

After a quick exchange of eye contact with my husband, I answer for the both of us. "You don't owe us anything. I love visiting Arizona, and we were able to get a refund for the retreat. It's a long story that I'm sure will be in every regional newspaper for the next week. I'd tell you to avoid the news, but I know you already do."

"Yeah. I find it easier to center myself if I don't focus on the negative. And the news is usually pretty negative. Again, super grateful." He presses his hands together in prayer pose and bows toward me. "Hey, you said something about a key?"

"Yeah, we searched the yurt where Greta had stayed, and I found a key she'd wrapped in a tie-dye scarf. Do you know if she had a safe deposit box or something like that?"

Dean leans back in his chair, takes the scrunchy from his hair, and scrapes it all back into a slightly fresher man bun. "No safe deposit box. She had a real thing about banks. There's no bus station in town, and I can't think of anything else with lockers."

Sinking into my extra senses, I pull the key out and attempt to get a reading. As the small silver key with its red plastic head rests in my palm, an employee walks by and points.

"Dude, are you a member of the health club? I love that gym. They have the best hot yoga classes in town."

A self-satisfied grin lifts my cheeks, and I glance toward my husband. "Do you feel like signing up for a gym membership, sweetie?"

He hangs his head and mumbles an affirmative.

"We're going to run down this lead, Dean. If there are any personal effects in the locker, we'll drop them off. Otherwise, we'll be heading up to the Grand Canyon and then we fly out tomorrow. I'm sorry I couldn't bring you better news, but I know there's a benefit to closure. At least I could give you that."

He slowly lifts his chin and looks deeply into my eyes. At first I want to look away, but I can sense how important this moment is for him.

"Mitzy, I know I'm not a great boss. I — I'm — I'm not even sure why you agreed to help me. If you ever need anything—"

Scooting to the edge of my seat, I lean forward and throw my arms around Dean. "Hey, we're all just humans doing the best we can. I'm truly sorry for your loss. Maybe take some time off work. Take the time you need to grieve. What you didn't know about her isn't important. The person you cared about, the person you gave your heart to, that's who you're mourning. Don't let anyone change that for you."

He returns the hug, and we all stand. As we walk out of the Brewed Dog, a little of my old supervisor surfaces. Dean calls out, "Have a super day."

We wave, return to our vehicle, and I give Erick directions to the health club.

"When we get there, we're going to have to pretend we want to sign up. They have a whole key-card system, and we'll need a cover story. You've got all the charm, so you keep the sales rep busy, and I'll pretend to inspect the equipment or something."

Erick parks, reaches for his backpack, and dumps the contents onto the back seat.

"Harper! What are you doing?"

"Whatever's in that locker, you're gonna need someplace to put it."

"Oooooh. Who's a sneaky little private investigator now?"

He winks and hands me the backpack. "You're a bad influence, Moon."

"I wouldn't have it any other way." Air kiss.

As he steps out of the vehicle, I call across the front seats. "Hey, take off that hoodie."

"Why?"

"Let's give them a peek at the guns, Detective Too-Hot-To-Handle. We're signing up for a gym membership, right? Well, you can be the gym rat, and I can be the charity case you're convincing to get healthy."

He laughs and tugs the hoodie off over his head.

When we reach the front door, the petite brunette sales assistant is opening the door before we even have a chance to pantomime our fake reason. She only has eyes for Erick.

Fine by me.

"How can I help you?"

"My wife and I are interested in signing up for a membership." Erick walks directly toward the desk and continues to fire questions at the gal.

I make use of the distraction and wander off in search of the lockers.

He's making adorable excuses for my behavior.

"Oh, ignore her. It's taken me a month to drag her down here. She has to look at all the equipment and make sure everything that's being raved about on social media is here. You and I can fill out the paperwork. She'll sign when she gets back."

It only takes a moment to locate the lockers. Pulling the key from my pocket, I search for number 49. When I insert the key and twist, it opens easily and I breathe a sigh of relief.

There's a duffel bag in the locker. I shove it into the backpack and feel around the inside for any hidden items that my extrasensory perceptions might detect.

Nada. Bupkus.

Copy that. Only a duffel bag, and I got it.

Returning to the front desk, I throw on my snarkiest, most spoiled voice and announce, "Sweetie, they do not have HIIT yoga. I can't even. I'll be in the car!"

And I push through the door and walk away.

Rest assured, Erick makes all the polite apologies before he follows in my footsteps.

Once he joins me in the Jeep, it's time to unpack the prize.

CHAPTER 24

My HUSBAND eagerly rubs his hands together. "All right, Moon. What've we got?"

Removing the duffel bag from his backpack, I set it on my lap and open the zipper. It's brimming with cash! "There's easily a hundred thousand dollars here."

Erick taps his hand twice on the steering wheel and grins with a hint of regret. "I was kinda hoping it wasn't true — the stuff Ethan told you."

"Yeah, me too. Although, we can definitely use these ill-gotten gains to make some wonderful additions to the Yavapai-Apache police vehicle inventory."

He nods and leans back in the driver's seat. "You can talk to Silas if you want, but I think we'll have to turn the money in."

"What? How would that do any good? There's no one to give the money back to, Harper. Why can't we use it for something positive?"

Erick sighs and shakes his head. "I know you like to bend the rules, Moon, but I can't budge on this one. We have to turn this money over to the proper authorities. I'm sure Arizona has a 'Return of Lost Property to Finder' rule, like most states. If no one claims it in the specified amount of time, it would be returned to us."

"That sounds like a lot of stupid red tape!" As I cross my arms and lean back in the seat, my clairsentience gets a hit of just how deep this conviction goes with Erick. The words of my wise grandmother echo in my mind, "You get more flies with honey."

"Fine — tabled for now. But you better call Silas and double check this Finder rule."

While Erick rings Silas to discuss our legal options, I continue to feel around the interior of the bag and check the two small outer pockets. When my hand stumbles across a thumb drive, I squeal with delight.

"Silas, I gotta go. Mitzy found something else."

Producing the thumb drive, I hold it up and waggle my eyebrows.

Erick grins broadly. "Are you thinking what I'm thinking?"

I return his smile and reply, "Almost never. But I'm thinking this might be some kind of blackmail material Greta was keeping as a failsafe against Ethan or Remiel. Let's head up to Flagstaff and hit the store on the college campus. I'll grab a laptop and we can see what's on this thing."

We enjoy a gorgeous and refreshing drive up the canyon. Bright sunlight filters through the towering pines, and the weather is as close to perfection as you can get in the Southwest.

With the windows down, we can feel the warm breeze and smell the hint of approaching fall weather. As we climb the switchbacks, my excitement grows. Something tells me this thumb drive holds the key to completing this case properly. It's not a psychic thing. I have had no confirmation from my mood ring, but I feel it — in my gut.

I direct Erick through the campus, and he parks outside the store.

"I'm running in to get a laptop. You stay here with the cash, all right?"

He nods once. "Got it."

The unsuspecting bookstore employee never made such a sale so quickly.

I take the laptop, a car charger, a backup battery pack, and anything else the gal tosses on the counter. Grabbing my sack full of hope, I race to the Rubicon and set up the laptop.

As soon as we have power, I plug in the thumb drive.

"Whoooo-ee, Harper."

He looks over my shoulder as I scroll through the contents. It contains a variety of files: PDFs, JPEGs, spreadsheets, and text documents.

It would appear that Greta never trusted Remiel for a minute. Not only does she have a spreadsheet of every account, but she also has copies of incriminating documents an eighteen-year-old Kyle signed as he tucked away the money he was skimming from his father. The money he claimed Ethan had stolen.

"Wow. This does not look good, Erick. If Kyle was this twisted at eighteen — maybe his father didn't commit suicide. Maybe Greta uncovered the truth and ran before Kyle could silence her too."

Erick scrapes his fingers through his tousled blond hair. "That's an open and shut case right there. We should turn this over to state's attorney, but if we—"

"If we hand over the cash, it will end up in evidence for eternity."

He rubs his left thumb along his stubbled jaw. "Yeah. Not turning it in isn't an option for me, though."

"Look, Harper, I hate to continue being a bad influence, but you and I are the only ones who know we recovered the money. This thumb drive could've been found on Greta's person, or it could be the thing that I found under the bed wrapped in the scarf!"

Erick chews the inside of his cheek and tilts his head from shoulder to shoulder. "Sorry, Moon. I gotta go with my gut on this one. We're definitely turning in the money."

All of my extra abilities are chiming like church bells. This is an opportunity to compromise. This relationship has to have give and take. Looks like it's my turn to give. "All right. I'll admit this would've been more of a rule break than a bend. We'll turn it in."

"Thanks, Moon." He leans toward my seat and kisses my cheek.

"Although, maybe we don't have to be the ones to tell the authorities. I can pass all of this along to Silas and tell him the options. BTW, what did he say about this money?"

"He said he'll meet us at the Flagstaff airport tomorrow. We'll hop on a plane and head home, and he'll take care of the things you want to do for the tribe via wire transfers from the Duncan-Moon Foundation."

"Yeah. That sounds great. He can turn in the money and the thumb drive. He'll know exactly how to present it to the authorities."

My partner sighs and slowly nods. "The most important thing is making reparations to the tribe that Kyle scammed."

Now that I've soothed Erick's nerves, I need to wrap up this southwestern adventure. I miss Grams and Pye.

"Based on the fact that we're carrying around about a hundred thousand in cash, I don't think you're going to get quite the tour of the Grand Canyon, you hoped. We'll drive along the south rim, and I'll show you some of the best scenic overlooks, but one of us will have to stay in the car at all times."

Erick nods. "Yeah. I understand." He leans toward me and kisses my cheek. "But don't think protecting a sack of cash is going to save you when the lights go out."

"What are you talking about?"

"I'm assuming you want to stay at a hotel in Flagstaff tonight? All I'm saying is, we'll bring the cash into the room. No one's staying in the car overnight."

Yeesh!

"Focus on your sightseeing, Harper."

He mumbles something salacious as he backs away from the campus store.

I super love this man!

. . .

OUR TRIP TO THE GRAND CANYON begins on a high note. The man at the gate asks Erick if he's a veteran, and we receive a lovely discount. However, things are a bit hit or miss after that.

As we travel the various scenic overlooks dotted along the south rim, we either have an opportunity to enjoy the magnificent vista stretching unbroken before us (*Hit*) or we struggle to find a parking spot and Erick has to jostle his way through busloads of tourists posing precariously on rocks, ledges, and guard rails. (*Miss*)

"Thanks for taking the time to show this to me, Moon. I'll never forget it."

"No problem, Harper. I've only seen it once before myself. We had a sixth-grade field trip here, and I barely remember anything. I love all the rock formations and the striations of color in the stone. It's gorgeous. But it seems to have turned into an over-the-top tourist attraction."

"I'd have to agree. The risks some of these people are taking in order to get the perfect picture for social media could end up going viral for all the wrong reasons."

My tendency toward dark humor allows for an unnecessarily loud gasp and a chuckle. "You know, there's actually a book about all the people who have died in the Grand Canyon. It's organized by type of death — that's how unbelievably high the numbers are."

Erick arches an eyebrow and shakes his head. "I guess it's a good thing you're the one staying in the car guarding the cash."

"What? Why?"

"Of the two of us, we both know who the risk taker is."

Oh brother.

As we exit the national park, Erick sighs wistfully. "What would you think about getting a cabin up here?"

"At the Grand Canyon? It's all national park." My face twists with confusion.

"Not right here." He laughs. "Maybe in Flagstaff or in the canyon — by the creek."

My heart swells with emotion. "You really like it here, don't you?"

"I feel connected to you — to your past — in a different way when we're in the AZ."

"Simmer down, Harper. Don't try to start sounding like a local with your 'AZ' nonsense. I'm not against the cabin idea, but I can't think clearly on an empty stomach."

He reaches across the center console and squeezes my knee. "Okay. You're off the hook for now, but I reserve the right to recall the topic, Your Honor."

"Yeesh!"

After a day of exploration, we stop off in the small town of Williams to have a slice of what's purported to be "the world's best pie," and, of course, french fries. But don't tell Odell.

"Is it the world's best pie? No. Is there enough whipped cream on the top to make up for that deficit? Yes."

Erick grins and licks the whipped cream off his lip.

Whew. It suddenly got rather hot in here. If that man knew how sexy he was, he'd be dangerous. I opt to change the subject rather than drool. "So we head back to Flagstaff, check into a hotel, and then what?"

"How about sushi for dinner?" He finishes his last bite of pie and grins.

"Not a fan. I had a less than stellar experience the first time I tried it. The ending pretty much soured me on the whole concept of eating raw fish."

"They have some awesome rolls that are all vegetable. I get this isn't your thing, but we promised each other we'd try new things, right?"

"I'm deeply regretting that promise right about now, Harper."

CUT TO —

Erick and I pacing outside Gate 10 at the Flagstaff airport. My stubborn mood ring finally flickers to life and encircles my left ring finger in a warm glow.

Glancing down, I see the unmistakable grey mustache of my mentor. And when I look toward the jetway door, the unmistakable bald pate, ruddy jowls, and fusty tweed coat appear.

"Silas! Silas!" I wave my arms wildly as though my snow-white hair isn't going to be beacon enough.

He shuffles toward us, and we lead him to a safe distance from the car rental counter.

"Good morning, Mizithra. I trust you slept well."

"Silas, we can dispense with the formalities. We have to get in line to go through the security checkpoint. Our plane leaves in less than an hour."

He harrumphs. "Proceed."

"Thanks. Here's the duffel bag. It contains the recovered money and the laptop I purchased. I copied all the files from the thumb drive onto the laptop, in case you want to *peruse* anything. The thumb drive has been wiped clean of all prints" — I glance at Erick and nod, giving him the credit he deserves — "and it's in a plastic baggie in this tiny front pocket of the duffel bag. Are you sure this will work?"

"Indeed. I shall check myself into a hotel this evening, and make a list of the local contacts I must rely upon to obtain the vehicles you requested. The scholarships must be handled separately. I will approach the appropriate tribal council members, and speak to them about what has transpired. Of course, I shall hand over this recovered cash to the proper authorities, while keeping things vague regarding how we have happened upon the funds."

Leave it to Silas to make something complicated sound downright impossible.

"I have complete faith in you, Mr. Willoughby." Without warning, he leans forward and embraces me. "Silas, you never—"

"Perhaps I've grown sentimental in my old age. Mr. Harper informed me of how close we came to losing you — once again. I'm afraid you've grown on me, Mizithra Achelois Moon. I fear I would be bereft if you were taken from us too soon."

Tears trickle down my cheeks and onto the rough fabric of his shoulder.

Erick rubs a hand across my back. "Hey, I don't want to break up this beautiful moment, but we've got a plane to catch."

"See you in Pin Cherry, Silas."

He smooths his bushy grey mustache with thumb and forefinger, and nods. "I shall look forward to it."

With that, Erick and I hustle toward the security line, which is thankfully short in this small regional airport. We checked our carry-on bags earlier, but we couldn't possibly go through security until after we met Mr. Willoughby and unloaded our sack full of cash.

I'm looking forward to Mr. Willoughby's return to Pin Cherry to fill me in on how everything turns out with the Yavapai-Apache tribe in Camp Verde. Erick and I decided a couple of quads, two police cruisers, a new bus, and at least two scholarships would be a great way to show our gratitude to Officer Vincent and his tribe.

"I can't wait to get home!"

Erick slips an arm around me and whispers in my ear, "Wherever you are is home for me."

CHAPTER 25

AFTER OUR LAYOVER IN CHICAGO, our puddle-jumper plane lands safely in Pin Cherry Harbor, and I'm eager to put my feet on *terra firma*.

However, my first instinct is to take my phone out of airplane mode and check my messages.

Mr. Willoughby, efficient as always, is ahead of schedule. He has already secured the bus and the quads. He's filed the necessary paperwork with the local authorities, and if the recovered funds are not claimed in ninety days they will revert to Silas Willoughby, and he will reimburse the Duncan-Moon Foundation.

My walk across the tarmac is all the welcome I need.

When Erick opens the door and I step into the airport, I discover the universe has other plans.

A banner and several cheering humans, all seeming to brim with joy, throw me off my game.

Odell, my father Jacob and his wife Amaryllis, my stepbrother Stellen and his girlfriend Yolo, Tally, Doc Ledo, and, shockingly, in the veterinarian's lap, Pyewacket. However, most astonishing is the presence of Twiggy. She actually missed me. I'm not foolish enough to point this out.

"Welcome back!" The shouts come from everyone at once.

I burst into tears while Erick picks a more practical approach. He thanks everyone and mentions my two giant suitcases that must be retrieved from baggage.

He jogs off to take care of business, and I make the rounds.

"Gramps, was this your idea?"

The wrinkles around Odell's eyes deepen and he grins sheepishly as he runs a weathered hand through his utilitarian grey buzz cut.

Tally answers for him. "You know your grandfather, honey. Silas mentioned all the trouble you two had gotten into out there in the Wild West, and Odell set this all up. But he'd never take the credit!" She slaps him on the back and chuckles.

Moving down the line, I hug each of my chosen, and actual, family members. My heart grows fuller with each embrace.

When I circle back, Doc Ledo rolls his wheel-chair forward to bring Pyewacket closer.

"Doc, is that a collar and a leash? How in the world did you—" I scan the veterinarian for claw marks and shockingly find none.

He points to the coiled leash in his lap and shrugs with mischief. "I told Pyewacket that if he wanted to greet you at the airport, he'd have to en-dure this indignity. However, I promised not to give it a single tug. We agreed that as long as he sat in my lap, he could retain his freedom."

Reaching forward, I scratch vigorously between my caracal's black-tufted ears. "I think I missed you most of all." As though he recognizes the para-phrased quote from *The Wizard of Oz*, I swear Mr. Cuddlekins chuckles.

My volunteer employee scoff-cackles, forcing me to ask a question I don't really want to have an-swered. "And how did the cleaning go, Twiggy?"

She flicks her grey pixie cut and it pains her to reply. "Silas kept the little demon spawn under con-trol. But next year he goes to the cabin — no matter how many corpses come calling."

Erick returns with the bags and helps me ex-tract myself. "Hey, I need to get Mitzy home to freshen up. Why don't we reconvene at the diner and enjoy slices of pin cherry pie all around?"

My stepbrother Stellen cheers the loudest. To be fair, he is a growing boy.

I sidle up next to my grandfather and whisper, "We ate at a restaurant in Arizona that claimed to have the world's best pie. It did not. Seems like Erick is trying to make it up to me."

Odell's heartwarming chuckle fills my soul to brimming, as he and I follow my favorite former lawman out of the airport.

And trust me when I tell you, this view beats anything the Grand Canyon has to offer!

End of Book 3

But, the mysteries continue...
Curl up with the next book in the Harper and Moon Investigations series!

A NOTE FROM TRIXIE

I love a good travel mystery, but it's always comforting to return home. Thank you for joining Mitzy and Erick on their new adventures in **Harper and Moon Investigations**. As always, I'll keep writing them if you keep reading . . .

The best part of "living" in Pin Cherry Harbor continues to be feedback from my early readers. Thank you to my alpha readers/cheerleaders, Angel and Michael. HUGE thanks to my fantastic beta readers who always give me actionable and honest feedback: Veronica McIntyre and Nadine Peterse-Vrijhof. And big "small town" hugs to the world's best ARC Team – Trixie's Mystery ARC Detectives!

My diligent editor Philip Newey definitely helped me straighten out a crooked timeline. Many thanks to him! I enjoy getting his notes and polishing each case. I'd also like to give tons of gratitude to Roxx at Proof Perfect for the wonderful proofing! Any remaining errors are my own.

FUN FACT: I've actually been in a sweat lodge — ONCE!

My favorite line from this case: "I've reached the end of my new-age macramé rope." ~Mitzy

I'm currently writing book four in the **Harper and Moon Investigations** series, *Fatal Wines and Valentines*. All your *Mitzy Moon Mysteries* series favorites will continue on — but there will definitely be a murder!

I hope you'll continue to hang out with us.

Trixie Silvertale (September 2023)

FATAL WINES AND VALENTINES

Harper and Moon Investigations No. 4

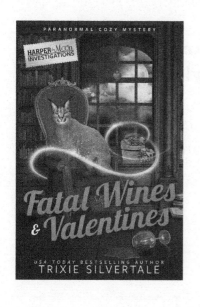

A Valentine's extravaganza. A crushing murder. Will our psychic sleuth uncork the clues before the wine turns blood-red?

Mitzy Moon is hoping to subtly celebrate the heart-filled holiday. She'd love a murder-free dinner with her hubby and a cute box of chocolates. But when a mysterious gilded invite arrives at her door, her simple plans could sour.

Ghost-ma threatens to haunt Mitzy into eternity if she skips the social event of the season. Dressed to the nines, the newlyweds head to the romantic gala. But instead of fine wines, they're faced with a shocking homicide and an overflowing list of suspects.

Can Mitzy and Erick burst a killer's bubble, or will this case take a deadly spill?

Fatal Wines and Valentines is the fourth book in the hilarious paranormal cozy mystery series, Harper and Moon Investigations, a spinoff from the popular Mitzy Moon Mysteries. If you like snarky heroines, supernatural intrigue, and a dash of romance, then you'll love Trixie Silvertale's perplexing puzzle.

Buy Fatal Wines and Valentines to bottle a murderer today!

Grab yours!
https://readerlinks.com/l/3454597

Scan this QR Code with the camera on your phone. You'll be taken right to the Harper and Moon Investigations series page. You can easily grab any mysteries you've missed!

Once you're in the Club, you'll also be the first to receive

updates from Pin Cherry Harbor and access to giveaways, new release announcements, short stories, behind-the-scenes secrets, and much more!

Scan this QR Code with the camera on your phone. You'll be taken right to the page to join the Club and get your FREE Novella!

THANK YOU!

Trying out a new book is always a risk and I'm thankful that you rolled the dice with Mitzy Moon. If you loved the book, the sweetest thing you can do (*even sweeter than pin cherry pie à la mode*) is to leave a review so that other readers will take a chance on Mitzy, Erick, and the gang.

Don't feel you have to write a book report. A brief comment like, "Can't wait to read the next book in this series!" will potential readers make their choice.

Leave a quick review HERE
https://readerlinks.com/l/3454580

★★★★★

Thank you, and I'll see you in Pin Cherry Harbor!

Mitzy Moon Mysteries

Heists and Poltergeists: Paranormal Cozy Mystery

Blades and Bridesmaids: Paranormal Cozy Mystery

Scones and Tombstones: Paranormal Cozy Mystery

Vandals and Yule Scandals: Paranormal Cozy Mystery

Harper and Moon Investigations

Bells and Bombshells: Paranormal Cozy Mystery

Rodeo Clowns and Shakedowns: Paranormal Cozy Mystery

Stiffs and Petroglyphs: Paranormal Cozy Mystery

Fatal Wines and Valentines: Paranormal Cozy Mystery

MAGICAL RENAISSANCE FAIRE MYSTERIES

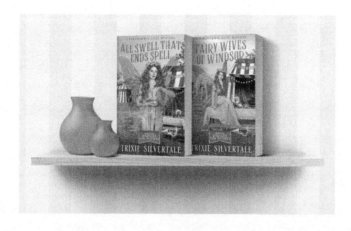

Explore the world of Coriander the Conjurer. A fortune-telling fairy with a heart of gold!

Book 1: ***All Swell That Ends Spell*** – A dubious festival. A fatal swim. Can this fortune-telling fairy herald the true killer?

Book 2: ***Fairy Wives of Windsor*** – A jolly Faire. A shocking murder. Can this furtive fairy outsmart the killer?

Book 3: ***Double Double Royal Trouble*** – When a treat-peddling witch is found dead, will this cursed faire crumble?

*Join Sydney Coleman and her unruly ghosts, as they solve
mysteries in a truly haunted mansion!*

Book 1: **Moonlight and Mischief** – She's desperate
for a fresh start, but is a mansion on sale too good to be
true?

Book 2: **Moonlight and Magic** – A haunted
Halloween tour seem like the perfect plan, until there's
murder...

Book 3: ***Moonlight and Mayhem*** – An unwelcome visitor. A surprising past. Will her fire sale end in smoke?

ABOUT THE AUTHOR

USA TODAY Bestselling author Trixie Silvertale grew up reading an endless supply of Lilian Jackson Braun, Hardy Boys, and Nancy Drew novels. She loves the amateur sleuths in cozy mysteries and obsesses about all things paranormal. Those two passions unite in her Harper and Moon Investigations, and she's thrilled to write them and share them with you.

When she's not consumed by writing, she bakes to fuel her creative engine and pulls weeds in her herb garden to clear her head (*and sometimes she pulls out her hair, but mostly weeds*).

Greetings are welcome:
trixie@trixiesilvertale.com

BB bookbub.com/authors/trixie-silvertale

f facebook.com/TrixieSilvertale

O instagram.com/trixiesilvertale

Made in the USA
Monee, IL
11 September 2023

42544288R00163